Black Picket

Black Picket

a novel

Ana Rêve

COYOTE CREEK BOOKS | SAN JOSÉ | CALIFORNIA

This book is a work of fiction. Names, characters, places, and incidents either are products of the author's imagination or are used ficticiously. Some modifications have been made with factual details in service of the story.

Printed in the United States of America.

25 24 23 22 21 20 19 18 17 16   2 3 4 5 6

Published by Coyote Creek Books.

ISBN-978-0-9964686-0-2

"The human race tends to remember the abuses to which it has been subjected rather than the endearments. What's left of kisses? Wounds, however, leave scars." - Bertolt Brecht

Prologue

When I think of my childhood, I think of enemas. The humiliation and discomfort of bending over the bathtub rim. The "please stop" implorations, followed by the fear of loss of control before she gave me privacy. The entire process shrouded as necessary before I could have a piece of candy. If I didn't "go" for three days, an enema was a must. It was the 1940s, and she was obsessed with bodily functions, and the control thereof. Early in my kindergarten year at P.S. 272 in Brooklyn, New York, she was called to school to pick me up. Mother was mortified. I was a timid, fearful child and had wet my pants. At the age of seventy, I still remember the "walk of shame" home. I can't recall her exact words, but the memory of the tone still haunts me. The gist:

"How could you disgrace me like that! You're a big girl now. What will the teacher say?"

Her obsession persisted throughout the years. When I was eight, at a family get together, my uncle accidentally walked into the bathroom while I was sitting on the toilet. I was duly distressed because of Mother's iron-clad rules of closed doors for dressing, undressing, and bathroom privacy, which I had unwittingly adopted over the years. I couldn't face my uncle for a long time. I remember Mother pretending to laugh about the incident. Telling others about it. Not soothing me, anything to avoid seeming incompetent about bathroom etiquette. Always worried about her public image.

My home was not a sanctuary. I was an only child. Perhaps siblings would have diluted Mother's intensity of control. Perhaps another child would have rebelled. Perhaps there is preprogrammed DNA that dictates how one reacts to negative or unreasonable parenting. Another child could have shrugged her shoulders and declared, "Whatever" or even the forbidden "No."

I am writing to exorcise my lingering demons, the memories and thoughts I was never allowed to share. I have chosen to rely on reminiscences. I have neither revisited the actual locations of my past, nor checked with relatives and friends. This is my official chronicle teeming with selective memory, in essence a work of autobiographical fiction. A coming-of-age tale, if you will.

Chapter 1

At what age does one actually remember an event, a feeling, or a mood? Did a parent repeat a story so often that it seemed true? Has one been shown a photograph that seems to corroborate a certain slant or interpretation?

My first smile, from the baby carriage, was thanks to a dog. To this day I owe a debt to canines and other critters. When times were bleak, I could always gain solace from a lick on the hand or a touch of a paw. One thing is certain. At the age of nine, I distinctly recall my exact words, begging my parents for a dog "so I wouldn't need people." I feel the same way today.

I was born in Brooklyn – Sheepshead Bay, near Coney Island. We lived on the fourth floor in an ordinary, unimposing apartment building in a one-bedroom unit. The living room window looked out at the water, docked boats, and gulls. There was a handful of trees across the street, and several blocks down a pedestrian bridge to Manhattan Beach. We lived down the street from Lundy's, the famous seafood restaurant.

As for my edifice, I remember a creaky elevator, a row of locked mailboxes, and a dark, scary basement. That basement contained a couple of stark rooms for the custodian, an area for a communal washer and dryer, and a storage space for trunks and bicycles. The passageways resembled a clandestine tunnel. I always felt nervous when we took a shortcut and walked underground to the temperamental lift.

I see myself at the age of four. The year was 1944, and my dad had enlisted in the army. He was going away to war. Mother was very upset. I didn't understand. Where was Europe? If it were dangerous, why was he leaving us? Daddy would no longer be able to scoop me up and take me to the carousel at the boardwalk. Dad was the one who gave me hugs and kisses. I knew he loved me. Now Mommy would be in charge.

Even at four, I knew it would be harder for me with him gone. Mommy was very strict and overly concerned about what others thought about her and her family. This applied to kith and kin and even strangers. She wouldn't even use the coin-operated laundry in the cellar because of an ill-defined sense of pride. As a show of higher respectability, she sent laundry out.

I knew that Mommy wasn't happy. I can't remember her showing me affection or celebrating joyous occasions when we were alone together. No special moments. I existed in a constant state of stress. To a four-year-old, it meant no mistakes, do as you're told, and, above all, never embarrass your mother in public.

I recall a disturbing incident from that year. Daddy was still overseas. Mother and I were returning from grocery shopping. It was getting dark. We rode the elevator up to our floor in tired silence. Having missed our bus, we'd done a lot of walking. When we arrived at the apartment door, it was slightly ajar. Mother switched on the lights. Furniture was overturned, drawers were emptied onto the floor, and several glass ashtrays were broken. Family pictures had been stomped on. Someone had come in from the roof through the kitchen fire escape. Mother hysterically called the superintendent and the police. I never felt safe after that, even after the locks were changed. For months I averted my eyes from that window; the recollection frightened me, but I wasn't allowed to cry if other people were around. No airing dirty laundry. Even if it were beyond your control. No showing weakness to others.

They probably had known Daddy was gone…

And then Daddy did come home, a year later, in 1945. He had contracted yellow fever or something like that. A medical discharge. Mommy and I were very excited. We waited in the lobby of the apartment building. For hours. My freshly-ironed dress was getting all crinkly. Prolonged anticipation had made me cranky. Way after my usual bedtime, Daddy finally walked through the door. So handsome and so elated. I ran to him, and he lifted me up in his arms.

"Daddy, I've missed you so much!" I shouted.

"I've missed you too," he replied.

"Mom gets the first kiss," she declared.

Daddy put me down on a bench and grabbed Mom. I didn't care. I was just happy that he was here. The long-awaited homecoming was reflected in the oval mirror over the wooden desk in the corner. A family reunited! A portrait of an American soldier returning home. Thinner, wearier, yet Daddy just the same. Several neighbors on the first floor joined in as a welcoming committee, telling me that I was such a lucky girl to have my father back.

Unfortunately, the war had changed Daddy, his perspective on life. At first, I noticed little things. When he didn't know I was watching, a look of sadness appeared in his eyes. His experiences had been so horrible that upon his return we were never allowed to have peanut butter in the house – it had been one of the army's staple rations. He didn't allow me to go to Hebrew school or even attend Sunday morning playtime.

"But why, Daddy? I want to go to Sunday school."

"Sorry, you can't."

"But I want to. There are stories and songs and snacks and…"

"Stop. In the war children were killed for no reason. I no longer believe in God."

He didn't change his mind. He felt that fate had its own agenda, with no place for prayer. It made me sad; I had heard that going to temple was so much fun.

Some activities remained the same. We still ate Nathan's hot dogs at the Boardwalk, watched sailors on leave ride the Cyclone, and rode the Ferris wheel together. But Daddy was always worried about money, making ends meet. Upon his return from Europe, he had gotten a low paying job as an entry level newspaper photographer.

Daddy began to focus on earning more money and someday moving us out of the city. He wanted Mommy, and especially her family, to respect him and be proud. The Depression had prevented him from pursuing higher education. A learned man, he felt self-conscious about his lack of secondary degrees, reinforced by Mother's, and her mother's, attitudes. My mother had been the only one in her family to continue studying after high school.

By the time I was in first grade, I knew I had to be a "perfect" child: always obeying and always receiving the highest grades in school. Having to please became a fear instead of an option. I felt that if I upset Mommy, she would tell Daddy, and then I would receive the strongest punishment: he wouldn't talk to me. For an hour or longer. That was the worst penalty of all, worse even than being spanked. When I felt that he had withdrawn his love, I was inconsolable.

In school that year, as I was lining up from lunch to return to the classroom, an eighth grade monitor caught me whispering to the girl behind me. She threatened to tell my teacher, who would tell my mother. I panicked. I pleaded, really pleaded with her not to say anything. I started to cry. I felt Mother would not love me anymore. I resolved to try harder, even though I was doing my best. I apologized to the upper-class monitor. No note was sent home.

Mother was unpredictable. However, she was constant in her need to be obeyed. I don't remember where we were going, but it looked like we were going to miss the bus. Mother grabbed my hand and urged me to run faster. I was already out of breath. "Mom, what will you do if I don't?" I called.

"I will box your ears!" she shouted.

I thought she was joking. "I dare you!" I was being funny and going along with the jest.

The next thing I knew – "Ouch!" A sudden smack. She had, indeed, boxed my ears in front of the bus driver who had been waiting for us to catch up. I never again made the mistake of thinking my mom had a sense of humor.

At seven, I learned to feign adult mannerisms because my dad's inner circle of friends was childless by design. I would sit in a living room quietly, afraid to interrupt, afraid to spill a drink, and even afraid to sneeze, thereby drawing attention to myself. In my thoughts I remember tall, non-smiling persons who might give me a pat on the head if I were well-behaved in the grown-up environment. Only speak when spoken to. No fiddling. No touching knickknacks. Smile once in a while. I considered my life as one all-encompassing test. When these adult visits were over, it was a relief to exhale freely, but not too freely. I had to perform for my parents too.

Sometimes Daddy would drink too much, and I would dread the ride home from a social visit. He was so irresponsible, making a fool of himself by giggling and seeing how many olives he could load in his martini. He always promised it wouldn't happen again. But it did. I was afraid of his loss of self-control. I didn't feel safe in the car, afraid he would swerve out of the lane. I could not abide Mother's tirades – she would shriek, "Be careful!" – but I knew in these cases she was right. He shouldn't have been driving. I closed my eyes in the back seat and wished to get home safely.

Where was that brother or sister to be my partner-in-crime, the crime being a harmless rebellion and defiance in lieu of a shiver and worry about these all-too-grown-up grown-ups, who were never without a Tom Collins in their hands? I got lost in the shuffle of their socializing.

I created an imaginary pal, Priscilla. Any time I thought of being naughty, like purposely spilling one of their drinks, or fake-hiccupping, I blamed her. But Priscilla's presence was short-lived. I guess disobedience – even the thought of it – wasn't in my nature. Too risky. Somehow my parents would know.

When I was nine, Daddy let me have a canary, my first pet. Her name was Maxine, changed from Max when she laid an egg and didn't sing. Only the male canary sings. She was delightful. I taught her to pull a balloon along the floor. I was so proud of Maxine. Unfortunately, avian knowledge had not advanced yet, and due to an inadequate seed diet, she had a short life. I truly loved that little bird who had not put any restrictions on our relationship. I finally felt needed, wanted, and in control of the happiness of another being. I could care for and love her unconditionally. Dad understood my attachment because his mother had adored animals. He told me that when Grandmother had returned from a hospital stay, her little dog flew down a flight of steps to greet her and jumped into her arms.

Several months after Maxine came into my life, I was hanging out in the courtyard with a few kids from the apartment building. After tiring of marbles, we were playing "doctor" as children will do. Two boys – one the superintendent's son – another girl, and I. It was quite innocent, a "show me yours, and I'll show you mine" sort of thing. Somehow I had a feeling that I shouldn't be participating, because Mother, who was so private about bodies, would probably not approve. So I really wasn't enjoying myself, but I couldn't figure out how to back out because it was one of my rare times interacting with other children. So I just waited for playtime to be over. Then we heard someone coming and ran away to our own apartments.

For three days, I worried that Mother would find out. I was so scared that someone would tell that I did the inexplicable. I confessed. I told her I had done something terrible, and if she promised not to tell Daddy, I would explain. She promised. After listening to a few sentences, she became hysterical. She kept asking me if "he had put it in." She was talking incoherently about babies and shame. I didn't understand. I was sobbing. But I knew that I had done something really wrong. I kept asking her to forgive me. She didn't respond. Then she broke her promise. She didn't even wait till Daddy came home from work. She called him at work, telling him to rush home.

Daddy didn't speak to me for two days. He always took Mother's side.

That was my introduction to the birds and the bees.

And it was the end of playing with the neighbor kids. Mother developed her own caste system, placing white collar professions at the top and blue collar at the bottom. The superintendent's son could not play with me again.

Despite our acute financial worries, Mother felt a keen sense of superiority based on educational status. The truth was that if one's status were to be measured by a paycheck, we would be in the superintendent's league. Money woes were a constant undercurrent in our daily life.

One day, at the checkout counter of the local grocery, Mother's check bounced. We found out about it a few days later. Mother was so embarrassed. The cashier had even tried to reassure her that these things happen all the time. But having to listen to words of comfort from the market's workers was an unbearable humiliation. She felt that even the bagging clerk could sense our dollar problem.

"Your dad is impossible." She turned to me, livid. Thereafter I felt like everyone was staring at us when we frequented the store. Embarrassment turned to dread.

Distraught, Mother tried to hide from her family our financial nightmare. There had been non-too subtle signs of trouble: a struggle for rent and only one toy for my birthday, chosen at F.A.O. Schwartz. I was overwhelmed by this landmark children's paradise and having to make a choice: the shelves were filled with all the new play things from dolls to Schwinn bikes. It was almost a tease to walk around this magical toyland. I couldn't make up my mind. I even tried *eeny-meeny*. Finally I chose a pinafored Heidi marionette with braids like mine. I could make her dance or rest and shake her head yes or no. I could be in charge. I could be the caring mother.

Dad was having trouble re-paying loans he had taken out just to make ends meet. We started receiving phone calls from collection agencies. We feared Mafia-type loan sharks, mysterious hang-ups.

Mother had a miscarriage around this time. Of course, she didn't talk about it. I didn't even know why she was going to the hospital. When she came home, she asked me if I wanted a baby sister or brother. Or was I happy being an only child and having all their attention? Somehow I knew that I had to choose just me. I had the savvy to know that was what Mom wanted me to say. More guilt. After a few days at home, Mother dropped a bombshell. I asked how she was feeling.

"Not good. I never really felt well again after your birth."

What was Mother saying? I didn't understand. *My* birth? That was almost ten years ago.

"What do you mean?"

"You were a breech delivery."

"What does that mean?"

"You were born feet first and things got messed up. End of conversation."

"Sorry," I mumbled and left the room to find Heidi and give her a hug.

A few months later, due to gynecological complications, she had to have a hysterectomy. There would be no more babies for Mother. No siblings for me. My life intensified under a fierce parental microscope.

That school year ended with a letter of praise from my fourth grade teacher – no honor certificates were available at that level. I ran home excitedly. En route, it started raining. I opened the letter, and the raindrops smudged some words. The content was glowing. I was ebullient.

Dear Mr. and Mrs. G,

Your daughter is a smart, wonderful student. It was a pleasure to have her in my class. You are very lucky to have her.

Mother chastised me for opening the letter addressed to her. Raindrops to teardrops. She didn't even say she was proud.

What could I do to please her? I didn't know. But I had to try. I continued to over study to obtain some iota of warmth.

During this time I still was given enemas – even more degrading the older I became. Why didn't I just lie and say my stomach was on track? The routine was the same. She would follow me into the bathroom, holding the warm water bag, pushing the nozzle of the tubing into my rectum, invading my naked body.

"Please stop, it's enough, Mother. Stop."

Sometimes she did. Other times she waited.

It's lucky I had the outings with Dad to think about. The brass ring on the carousel, Brooklyn Dodger games at Ebbets Field, horse shows at Madison Square Garden. I knew he loved me.

Mother received a certificate from a teacher training school before she was married, so she could have gone back to the classroom at any time. But Dad was adamant that she not work in order to be at home for me, even though we needed money. He wanted to be the sole breadwinner, a proud man living up to the image of the times. It was one of the few times he put his foot down. And Mother obeyed.

Dad failed in a business venture opening his own studio, a project financed by his brother. He continued drinking a little too much. Each month it was a struggle to pay the eighty dollars rent-controlled fee. Mother had always smoked, but she slowly became a chain smoker. It was common to hear her berate him about the financial loss. She was embarrassed that Dad hadn't succeeded.

"What were you thinking?"

"I just wanted more for our family," he would answer.

"Now all we have is more debt."

Sometimes I tried to intervene and stick up for him. I didn't understand the money problems.

"Mom, I love Daddy," I would say.

"You always stick up for him. Peas in a pod."

She put him down the same way again and again. Eventually I just kept quiet.

Mother's oversensitivity must have started way back in high school. She would always tell the anecdote about the time the eleventh grade teacher called her up to his desk and asked her if she had had banana for lunch. She asked him, blushing furiously, "How did you know?" For in fact, banana was part of her daily brown bagging.

He replied, gently teasing, "Because there's skin all over your face."

Instead of laughing with her classmates at the joke – which could have been directed at anyone, really – she felt put down because of her inexpensive lunch. Now everyone, she worried, would know she couldn't afford tastier items: pastrami, tongue. She'd have to keep eating alone.

In school, I took a series of exams, including an IQ test, to see if I was qualified to skip the sixth grade and go straight to junior high. We were given a test to see which students could handle an advanced curriculum in lieu of remaining in elementary school. I overheard my parents talking about how important it was to them, especially since a cousin of mine had passed with flying colors at another school. I was so nervous that I had a mental block during the exam. I still can't remember what the format was. Mother couldn't accept the fact that I had not qualified. I overheard her talking to Dad in their bedroom. They thought I was asleep.

"What a mess. We need an explanation for her not making the cut."

"Don't worry about it."

"Keep your voice down; she'll hear us. I think I've got it. How does this sound: the principal was so pleased with her academic performance that he wanted to keep her in the K-8 to help in the office with attendance and delivering messages."

I let Mother down again. Why couldn't I do anything right? After a while, she actually believed her version of the test results.

I didn't want to be a student aide; in my heart I still knew I had failed. I wanted out of that school. Then maybe the feeling of failure would disappear. Along with my gawkiness, I wore glasses, was called "four eyes" by my peers. I developed a lazy eye, when one eye is much weaker than the other and stops working. I had to wear a patch over my good eye. Now I was "one-eye."

I started eating Fig Newtons for solace. A lot of Fig Newtons.

Mother was never emotional, didn't give hugs, or stray kisses; but if I pleased her with a perfect report card, which brought honor to the family, she would reward me with a subdued smile. And Fig Newtons.

I also found comfort in icing from the tops of cupcakes and muffins, chubby me. I envied the skinny cheerleader types.

I was tall for my age, and unpopular. We were weighed with the scale in full view of everyone during P.E. At one hundred twenty-two pounds, I was called "thunder thighs" by my classmates. I was the last chosen for teams. Recoiling from sports, I spent most of my recesses with a book. I was shy; my classmates considered me snobby and a loser.

Eighth grade sent me over the top of self-doubt. I developed a problem with facial hair. Even today when I hear "mustache" jokes, I am transported back to days of intense self-consciousness that persisted until I sought electrolysis treatment as an adult. These were the days before laser treatments and openly-discussed cosmetic techniques. Mother decided she could help and bought some facial wax. Somehow she had not followed the instructions carefully enough. The wax, when heated, started dripping down and formed what looked like an old-fashioned handlebar mustache. To my amazement, Mother started laughing. I started weeping, feeling betrayed and vulnerable. I tried to refrain from seeking her help with other ongoing puberty problems. I just winged it and said I understood or I knew. But I lied.

The summer vacation of my fourteenth year consisted of sitting with my mom under a tree across the street from our apartment building, the breeze cool from the bay an escape from the hot apartment. I read library books. It was all the vacation we could afford, a folded chair under a sidewalk tree.

That particular summer was also marked by high drama in our

apartment building. As per custom at the time, husbands drove their wives and children to the mountains, stayed for the weekends, then came home for the work week alone without their families. It was considered quite selfless of them. However, whispers among neighbors confirmed that three men had hired "a floozy" to stay in one of their apartments when households were temporarily vacated. To share her, no less.

I didn't understand so I asked Mom. She said, "I'm not surprised. Most men are not to be trusted. Some men are like that. Your dad would never do such a thing."

"But Mom, what does 'share' mean? Share time with her? Watch TV? Why is it called a scandal?"

"S-E-X," Mother spelled, awkward about saying the word.

Subject closed. But not for me. The men weren't selfless at all, as I had thought; they were sneaky and willing to betray their loved ones.

Around the same time a cousin came to visit with her new fiancé. In front of other relatives, Mother prefaced the introduction of him by saying how uneasy I would be. I couldn't imagine what she meant. Mother suggested that I ask him what he did for a living.

Naively I queried, "What's your job?"

He answered, "I promote dispensers of sanitary napkins in public restrooms."

My cheeks burned; I blushed intensely. All eyes turned to me, and once more I felt awkwardly self-conscious about my lack of composure when it came to bodily functions. I just knew Mother was chuckling.

Chapter 2

Sunday lunch at a restaurant was an inviolable ritual. Even in dire financial straits, eating out once every weekend was sacrosanct. I knew it was important, but I could never be sure if it was the food itself or my parents' desire to be seen in a refined setting—which culminated in the "Orthodontist versus Eating Out" debate.

My parents were told that I needed braces. Orthodontia wasn't a given then. After a few days deliberation, my parents decided not to correct my teeth; it was too expensive. I felt that my needs were secondary to their palates…or image. At the same time, I chided myself for being selfish. Who was I to deprive them of so important a pleasure? I added crooked bottom teeth to my list of negative attributes.

I'm sure that this restaurant obsession contributed to the onset of my anorexia at the age of thirty, although my stygian marriage pushed me over the edge.

The highlight of freshman year in high school was the fulfillment of my dream. One night in early September, Dad brought home a puppy – a fox terrier. I didn't know much about training, housebreaking, or being Alpha. But, I had plenty of love to spare. Rocky – named after Rocky Road ice cream – tugged on the leash, never attended obedience school, and was so happy to ride in the car that he tore all the seat covers. When I didn't get asked to join a sophomore sorority, I still had Rocky. When I was called "bookworm," I still had Rocky. When I suffered during an oral presentation, I still had Rocky. When I walked to the front of the room, I could see some of the girls raise their eyes to the ceiling, as if to say, "Oh no." Others giggled when I stumbled out of nervousness. They passed notes and looked bored. I was all too aware of being outside the inner circle.

In my junior year, my social studies teacher tried to get me to participate more in public speaking by threatening me with a maximum grade of 85% if I didn't improve my oral presentations. Even the fear of my parents' reaction couldn't make me tolerate additional scrutiny by my classmates. I was just as afraid that the class would mock me as I was of getting lower grades.

My weekends were bearable; there were even a few arranged dates thanks to well-intentioned neighbors in my mother's bi-monthly Mah Jong group. I can still hear the clicking of the tiles amidst the chatter. Mother was on her best behavior. She spent hours preparing delicious refreshments when it was her turn to hostess. Dad and I would try to make ourselves scarce at these times. One of her cronies had a nephew who was preparing to enter Brooklyn Downstate Medical College. This made him a real catch. I was pushed into a blind date.

We went to a James Dean movie, stopped for Cokes, and parked near the boardwalk, a popular make-out spot. He was sort of okay, but I wanted to go home. I wasn't attracted to him and wasn't looking forward to the obligatory necking. I felt shallow because I was very self-conscious of the fact that he was several inches shorter than I. I felt ashamed enough about my own body. I'd rather be reading with Rocky at my side. But I thought I owed him something for the evening. I didn't expect anything for myself.

The backseat was squishy and bumpy. I tried small talk to distract him. "How did you know you wanted to be a doctor?"

"I come from a family of MD's. It was expected of me. No more talking please."

He started to unbutton my blouse. He squeezed my boobs.

"Ouch. Stop, okay?"

"Too late."

He pushed me back against the seat, his erection on my stomach. He started to masturbate and handed me a handkerchief. In less than a minute he ejaculated into it. Safe sex. I had read a Health Ed book and at least knew what was happening. It was the first time I had felt the sticky stuff. I counted to fifty, disentangled myself, and asked to be taken home, where I threw the wet hanky down the incinerator.

Mother was disappointed when I told her that I wouldn't go out with him again.

On the Saturday before Christmas vacation in my senior year, my parents and I were scheduled to attend a French award ceremony. I had been encouraged to enter a contest and had won recognition. I didn't want to go to the assembly; the ceremony was taking place in Manhattan, which would mean taking the train and leaving Rocky alone for several hours. If I had so chosen, my French teacher would have picked up the prizes for me – copies of *Jeanne D'Arc* and *Paris in Our Time*. I had no problem with that. However, my parents did. They wanted the public recognition and the affirmation from society of my foreign language expertise. So I bought Rocky a new rubber ball to enjoy while we were gone.

When we arrived home, the prize books in my hands, Rocky wasn't at the door to greet us. He was sick. He had ripped the ball apart and swallowed a huge piece. In spite of surgery, he died at the age of three, two days later. I was beyond devastated at having lost the one being I truly loved in the family. I couldn't bear coming home without Rocky's welcoming bark and gyrations. I became a zombie. I kept to my routine: school, homework, eat, sleep. Out of body, I observed my hollow self. I was an empty shell.

A week after Rocky's demise, I fell ill, developing a high fever, extreme fatigue, and lethargy. The doctor couldn't figure out why I was so sick. Rocky had been the only one who kissed me; he made it okay that I didn't have friends. Perhaps the sickness was linked to the guilt I felt for buying the rubber ball, a classic example of the mystical connection between mind and body. The physical pain assuaged my mental anguish. In a strange way, I felt better emotionally, after having suffered physically for ten days. Penance. If only I hadn't chosen that dog toy…

It was almost time for the college acceptance letters to arrive. A fat envelope? You knew you'd been accepted, and there were forms to fill out. A slim envelope meant rejection. Dad was still struggling financially. However, it was his vicarious desire to have me accepted at an Ivy League college. I wanted to go to Barnard in New York City and commute from home so I could get another dog. Dad wanted me to hobnob with society. To each his own dream.

I prayed that I would be accepted at Barnard, even meriting a New York State scholarship to help with the tuition. I prayed some more that I wouldn't be accepted at the exclusive Ivy League Seven Sister College in New England. No such luck. My bulky envelope arrived. Dad was ecstatic that I was the first from my public high school to be admitted to this particular private institution. Several months later, since I ranked third in a class of twelve hundred students, I was chosen to participate in a valedictorian panel at graduation to be held at a local movie theater. I was a nervous wreck. Public speaking was forever nightmarish. Awkward and unpopular, no canine companion, no memories of a prom date.

My parents gloried in the presentation. Dad grinned and teared-up. He had his arm around Mom's shoulders. She was sitting up straight, not touching the back of the seat. There was a hint of a smile on her face as if to say, "I expected no less." When I met up with her after the ceremony, she said, "We're so proud of you."

Dad congratulated me with a hug. Mother gave me a partial hug and took my arm as we exited the theater.

I agreed to attend a July summer session at McGill University in Montréal. If Rocky had still been alive, I would not have left him to take any course. My parents wanted me to have an "away-from-home experience" before starting college in the fall and to get a head start on my major. The course required us to speak only French for six weeks in class as well as in our dormitories. I wanted to escape the memories of Rocky.

What I remember most from that summer was my panicky call to my parents. I wanted to take the courses pass/fail. That way I could remove the pressure of exams and try to enjoy myself. Their response was an unequivocal "No!" They paid good money, and they wanted grades. So I skipped the field trip to Québec City. I studied. I didn't date. I kept to myself. I earned my high grades.

When courses ended, my parents drove to McGill to bring me home. To celebrate my stellar report card, my family held a celebratory lunch at a Montréal French restaurant. They'd asked me to invite a friend; I had sort of befriended a Canadian classmate so I invited her.

Was it epicureanism or conceit? Dad was a genial host, the meal was a lavish offering, and my guest was duly impressed. My parents' patterns were unwavering.

My preparation for the Ivy League was dictated by the college issue of *Seventeen* magazine; I had never rubbed shoulders with an Ivy Leaguer. Neighbors and cousins matriculated at Brooklyn College and commuted from home. My future campus was too far away to visit in advance. There was no way to assess the privileged milieu. I so wanted to fit in. I bought the obligatory camel's hair coat thinking that it would solidify my acceptance. We pretended that I was a suburban Long Island Jewish Princess, when in fact I didn't even have my own space in our tiny Brooklyn apartment.

Seventeen featured beatific images of New England foliage, young men and women hand in hand walking towards an ivy laden building. I purchased all the required accoutrements, shoes and blouses, but at great emotional and financial cost. I wasn't skinny or attractive like the magazine co-eds. Mother, who was teaching part time, had some money and contributed to my trunk contents – with her usual tinge of envy.

I realized as I got older that Mother was jealous of Dad's love for me. Perhaps jealous is too strong a word. I felt she saw me as competition for Dad's attention. She resented our time together, whether to Luna Amusement Park or walks to see the fishing boats docked with their catch for the day.

"Don't bother waiting for me," Mother dismissed us. "Just go."

I knew she resented spending the money for my collegiate paraphernalia. Armed with the tools to mask the real me, I started to dread the end of August. Somehow I knew this would not be a fairy tale.

The rest of that summer passed quickly. During this time, Mother encouraged me to date, to prove that I would be popular as well as smart. Her date of choice, no matter what, would be any guy who was associated with an elite men's college. There was one particular Ivy League blind date before my matriculation. He was scheduled to commence his freshman year at the neighboring prestigious male institution. I assumed that he was entitled to remove my bra and "feel me up." I wasn't "busty" enough for him. He really wasn't interested, a foreshadowing of major hurt to come.

My final summer fling was with a Brooklyn guy, two years my junior, not an Ivy Leaguer, whom I met at the beach. At the very end of August, he placed his penis in my hand and pompously declared that that was what I needed.

All I needed.

The ultimate panacea.

It would solve all my problems.

I resolved to stop jerking boys off. For real this time. Too tedious and definitely a waste of time.

Summer ended. My college years had arrived.

Chapter 3

I knew I was in trouble at orientation.

The campus was New England at its best. Magnificent grounds reeking of learnedness amidst bountiful and loving nature. Rolling hills, a lake, and a quintessential variety of dorms, some old, some new. Groups of girls, enthusiastic girls, being greeted by upper-class women. Proud parents helping with luggage and newly-purchased trunks. Assignments of Big Sisters from the junior class, to entering freshmen. Immediately I became uneasy; everyone else seemed acquainted. A lot of hugging was going on. A junior asked if I had brought my horse with me to board nearby while attending college. A horse?

My roommate had not yet arrived. My parents helped me set up my side of the room, then prepared for the drive home. There would be a welcoming dinner in the dorm that night. I put on a happy façade when Mom and Dad drove away. In truth, I felt abandoned.

During that weekend of orientation, the highlights for me were the library and the bookstore. Books had always comforted me; solitude in the library cubicles was familiar and soothing. I clung to the written word instead of interaction with students. Dorm meals were particularly stressful as I floundered in small talk about cars and boyfriends. Others compared notes about trips abroad to far-off beaches, sailing. I sat there outside the golden circle, feeling ignored, removed from my urban community. They were polite but not so interested in being my friend. I didn't push it. There was to be a freshman mixer the following Friday night, and the girls were all atwitter about the event. I didn't know what to wear; I just hoped I would be asked to dance. I didn't want to be a wallflower.

I didn't know that popularity for the social was determined in advance. The bustier girls were the top choices at the opening mixer. All of us in the "A" cup category fell to the bottom of the marauders' dance cards.

It turned out that the junior class at the nearby brother school, as a traditional prank, had stolen my entering freshman class's "posture pictures" from the gymnasium office. Posture pictures, like an x-ray checking the curvature of the spine, were taken to assess whether or not a particular P.E. course would be beneficial. I was so aghast at the situation that I don't remember if we were allowed to keep our bras on. I left the festivities early. My first of many non-*Seventeen* moments.

We had all been assigned a roommate, supposedly based on common interests. My roommate was a nightmare: rich, snobbish, assertive, and a smoker. She was savvy about social mores. The school must have taken into consideration that we were both Jewish. She was nouveau riche with a forceful personality. I was the shy, slightly overweight girl from Brooklyn. She ridiculed me because I didn't know how to play Bridge or knit, and because I didn't join in for a nightly snack of graham crackers and milk. The boys with "Jr." and "The Third" attached to their name were not in my range, but they were in hers because of her family's wealth – she flaunted her elaborate sweet sixteen ball, with orchestra, formal gowns and tuxedos, and gourmet repast.

We tried to avoid each other, she a late-nighter, I an early riser. We lasted until the second semester when I moved into a single.

So I studied; there was plenty to study. Dorm life was not for me. Giggling, gossipy groups of girls who had grown up with overnight camp experiences and elaborate vacations to the Hamptons were closed to me. I, who had never stepped out of the insulation of my Brooklyn upbringing, was too nervous about my studies to work on gaining acceptance.

My sophomore year, I found a friend who became my roommate. She was a Jewish only-child from the Bronx. Her parents adored her – that was obvious from the hugs and kisses and goodies when they visited. She had a boyfriend, soon to become fiancé, who made the drive from New York every other weekend. My roommate was secure and confident. I was amazed that she didn't even wash her hair when her beau drove up. According to *Seventeen*, she was doing everything wrong.

We felt comfortable together, having attended large public high schools and having come from middle-class backgrounds. She was not pretentious. Still I never was able to enjoy the camaraderie, be it staying up late or leaving campus to party every weekend at a neighboring male college. My anxiety over tests and papers reasserted itself. I couldn't take grades casually. The "gentleman's C" theory did not apply to me. I had to excel. My roommate was more relaxed about academics. I felt she must be so secure because she had a steady boyfriend. Or understanding parents.

I chose French as a major. French literature to be exact, my dad's first choice. He had been in France during the war and had come to admire the French people. In my studies I got caught up in fictional grand passion and romance. I was assigned a paper analyzing Flaubert's Madame Bovary's adultery and its consequences. I still recall that Flaubert likened Madame B's husband to an ordinary cap, and I sympathized with her decision to follow her heart. The professor gave me a C and wrote on my essay that I had a lot of living to do before I could comment on these types of affairs.

I became carried away with enthusiasm for French novels; I moved on to wishing I could join the clique in my field who were chatting nonstop about spending junior year abroad. In France. In Paris. The foreign exchange program was a coveted one. On a Sunday in November, I called home excitedly.

"I have some great news. There's a program to spend junior year abroad and live with a French family. Most of my fellow majors are going to go. May I accompany them?"

Mother abruptly replied, "Absolutely not."

"Please? It would really make me happy. And it would perfect my French accent." I had been struggling in the oral practice lab with rolling my R's, gargling with water and still sounding like I was speaking French with a Brooklyn accent. "Please."

I waited for a yes. I could just imagine Mother's face with pursed lips and exaggerated frown.

"Let me be clear. I've never been to Europe. You can't get there first. I only take car trips to the Catskills and Adirondack Mountains. People would think it's strange."

The call ended in an abrupt cough. "Don't bring it up again."

I called back the next day, playing the grade card. "Please reconsider. It would help with my oral French."

"No, it's not fair that you get your wish while I stay home." She slammed down the phone.

I returned to my dormitory with a heavy heart. I worried that I would lose my academic prowess in my major to the lucky travelers. And they did come back remarkably fluent.

The highlight of junior year was the annual father-daughter dance, much anticipated and widely renowned. It was the popular event, publicized all around campus. I made certain that I stayed ahead of my academic commitments so I could be free of scholastic worry. It would be one of the few dances where I would have a date, and a handsome one at that. Dad was driving up from New York. We had planned to meet at a local motel on Friday night. I quickened my step as I approached his room. I knocked softly a couple of times. I heard his footsteps and smiled.

"Dad, here I am!" I cried.

"Coming."

When I heard his voice, I breathed a sigh of relief. I had been worried he wouldn't make it on time. There were short welcoming programs – slideshows highlighting college life including a tour of the library, stables, and lake – arranged before the big Saturday night spectacular.

Imagine my astonishment when the door opened and I saw Dad – and, behind him, Mom, greeting me. For a moment I was speechless.

"Mom, what are you doing here?" The words just burst from my mouth.

"What a nasty welcome. How rude!" She was so angry I hadn't reacted with delight at her appearance.

"But, Mom, this weekend is for fathers and daughters only. It's tradition. How can I break the rules? They'll be mad. Besides, what will you do while Dad and I are together?"

"I'll accompany you and Dad and watch the festivities from the sidelines. I have no intention of spending the weekend alone. I have every right to be here. I'm helping with your tuition. And there's no way I'm going to spend a boring weekend while you and Dad are having fun."

Saturday afternoon, wearing a sour expression, Mother walked along with Dad and me as we watched the competitive horse jumping and rowing. I was so aware of her negative presence that I couldn't enjoy the exhibitions, not even the equestrians.

Saturday night the gym was crowded and alive with music. Dad was quite debonair and a sharp dancer to boot. Many a girl whose father couldn't attend tried to cut in, especially when "Georgia on My Mind" played. They wanted to be dipped by him; he was an excellent dipper. Mother stood on the sidelines and glared. My night was ruined. I kept waiting for someone to ask why my mother was there.

Two weeks later, I received a care package from Mom, filled with Fig Newtons. These cookies became Mother's traditional way of saying perhaps-I-shouldn't-have-done-it, that she had a few regrets about her behavior.

College dating was not as successful as my studies. At that time, in the early Sixties, if one weren't "pinned" by senior year and intending to receive a Ph.T. ("Putting Hubby Through graduate school"), one had failed abysmally.

A sampling of forays in search of elusive popularity will illustrate my naïveté in the social scene:

Foray Number One. I was finally invited to a weekend away in Boston by a guy I met while indulging in a Cherry Coke and muffin, instead of dorm food, at the local campus inn. Handsome and glib, he sat down next to me, and I soon learned that he had been a leader in a Hillel group as an undergraduate. We began talking about being Jewish in a WASP environment. I felt that we had a great deal in common.

It was exciting to be asked by this Harvard pre-law student from Pennsylvania to watch him participate in an important mock trial on the upcoming Saturday morning. He would be up against elite adversaries, la crème de la crème. He had been preparing for weeks. It would be my first time in the inner sanctum of academia, a.k.a. Harvard Law School. Now I could join the mass weekend exodus. My parents would be overjoyed; Mother could boast about how popular I was and that I had been asked to spend a weekend in Boston, at Harvard no less.

When I got off the bus on that Saturday morning, Pre-Law was confidence personified. I felt proud as we entered the hallowed auditorium. I wished him luck. He remarked that he wouldn't need it; the win was in the proverbial bag.

Nevertheless, I would provide moral support. The debate on the topic of constitutional rights became intense. He lost. He lost dismally.

A weekend of sulking ensued throughout a play, throughout meals, even throughout a Sunday Harvard Medical School lecture on hysteria. I found the presentation quite interesting, especially the appearances of actual patients. One case in point: someone who couldn't see after witnessing a horrendous traffic accident. The trauma had made him blind.

My date was still adrift of his own unwonted defeat. It even affected him in the bedroom while we were making out. At that time, the early Sixties, a "good girl" didn't go all the way; she waited until marriage. There was an all-encompassing fear of pregnancy and being ostracized. You could sleep over, one over the quilt, one under. Mutual masturbation was tolerated. Necking, neck up, petting, waist down. Everything but intercourse. But my elite date could not be roused from his depressive state. Deflated egos, deflated desires. So much for romance in an intellectual setting.

Foray Number Two. I was invited to spend Saturday and stay overnight in Darien, Connecticut at a classmate's house. There would be a small get together with her friends in the evening and the prospect of a blind date. Driving over to swim at a country club, we were three couples squished in a station wagon. My maybe-blind date seemed to be in a jovial mood.

"Hey guys! Great Saturday weather for swimming."

The driver replied, "Yeah, we can rest tomorrow on the Sabbath."

My maybe-blind date chuckled. "But you know, the rabbi wouldn't allow driving today."

I started to feel uneasy. The driver continued. "Well now, which is the true Sabbath, Saturday or Sunday? Everyone?"

Then I understood. Jewish orthodox practice was being used as the punchline of a prejudicial joke.

My maybe-blind date thought the question was hilarious.

My classmate remained silent.

We arrived at our destination. Any enthusiasm I harbored for this jaunt had dissolved. But nothing had prepared me for the reception I received. Or rather didn't.

We all had to sign in, even the guests, at the front desk in the lobby. I could hear the sounds of splashing and water play. There was a refreshment area to the right. My spirits rose a little, but not for long.

When I entered my name in the daily log, my surname – Goldberg – drew a pause from the receptionist. She telephoned for her superior who sheepishly informed me that the guest quota was filled for the day.

I had grown up sheltered in a New York melting pot environment. Now I went into shock and didn't know how to handle the situation.

I'm embarrassed to admit that for the rest of my college career, when asked, I changed my hometown from Brooklyn (New York) to Brookline (Massachusetts). I dropped the "berg" from my name and avoided all private clubs.

I recalled this incident with a jolt when Sammy Davis, Jr., one of the popular Rat Pack, joked that since converting to Judaism, and being Jewish as well as Black, he would no longer be welcome in Darien.

Foray Number Three. I had a few dates with a track enthusiast from Yale. He wasn't the man of my dreams, but he was halfway decent, and an Ivy Leaguer. He had promised to see me over the summer, so I told him I would be working as a counselor for three- and four-year-olds at Pinedale Inn in the Catskill Mountains, a popular resort area for Jewish families. Things were going well for me – I loved the kids – until I was reprimanded for making up a story at naptime about a bunny who ate lamb chops and drank too much milk for dinner. The head counselor called me in to the rec room to remind me that Pinedale was a kosher resort, and therefore one would never serve meat and dairy at the same meal. I was duly disciplined and threatened with losing my job if it happened again. Imagine my happiness when Yaley called me early morning one Friday and said he would drive over for a date that evening. I really needed that ego boost. I knew my mother would be proud of the fact that a pedigreed Yaley would make the effort to see me. Deep down I couldn't believe it was true.

It wasn't.

When I heard my name over the loud speaker at four o'clock to come to the reception desk, I had a feeling something was wrong. Yaley was canceling, feigning he had forgotten a former commitment. I surmised that his parents had found out about the Catskill Jewish connection and, as Catholics, had forbidden him to come. I really wasn't surprised. I had to pretend he had had a family emergency when several of the staff asked me where my date was. Reality had reared its ugly head.

Foray Number Four. At Pinedale Inn, I met a charming guy who was waiting on tables at the Inn to help pay for his college tuition. He was matriculated at the engineering graduate school in Rochester. And he was Jewish. After returning home in late August, I saw him twice before my senior year started. We danced to "I Only Have Eyes for You" and "There Were Bells on the Hill." He told me that he had to stay at school over Christmas break to work on his major project. Would I fly up to visit him?

I had been indoctrinated: a holiday date meant you were popular; alone on Christmas or New Year's Eve, you were a loser. Finally I felt like I was in a winter festival romance. My parents were delighted because they could boast of my well-rounded collegiate image. I wasn't just a bookworm. I didn't tell them he was from the Bronx, and feigned that he resided on Long Island. In the interim, I was determined to lose the twenty-five pounds I had gained, thanks to constant stressful academic pressure, in order to surprise him in December—even though he had said that he preferred more of me to love. I wasn't sure I believed that.

I got down to one hundred twenty-four pounds – throwing away many Fig Newtons Mother had sent – and felt more attractive than usual. I was learning the art of control. Somehow the feeling of being hungry was becoming more comfortable than being sated.

I crossed off the days until December 22. I pictured running towards him, in a William Holden *Love is a Many Splendored Thing* reenactment.

The plane landed. Charming was waiting at the terminal. I had forgotten how cute he was, my own private Gregory Peck. I catapulted into his arms. It was an awkward embrace; he was holding a dozen yellow roses. He gave me a clumsy bear hug while kissing my eyes, nose, and working his way slowly to my mouth. He removed an adorable stuffed Snoopy from inside the bouquet. We walked out hand-in-hand into slush. Rochester was cold and snowy. Very cold. Very snowy. But I hardly noticed.

When we arrived at his apartment in a decrepit, abandoned-looking building, he led me up a dingy staircase and opened his door. It was a characteristically rundown college accommodation. The ramshackle furniture was beyond tacky. I felt a little spooked, maybe because we were the only occupants in the house due to the fact that it was a few days before Christmas. The majority of students had already returned home for the holidays.

The tour ended abruptly in the bedroom. Rather than sparking fanciful romance, my weight loss had incited his unbridled lust. I was thrown, rather unceremoniously, on the bed. I tried to diffuse the moment by talking to him.

"Hey! What's going on? Let me up," I began to plead.

"It's party time. Two fun-filled days," he replied.

"What do you mean two days? I thought we were spending the week together."

"Are you kidding? I'm going home on Monday for the holidays."

I couldn't believe it. My mind rejected the implication that I had been cunningly deceived. A bombshell. And now I had to deal with unwanted, frightening, rude lust.

I wanted to go home. Right away. Even if I had to call my dad to meet me at the airport in New York that very same night. Even if that meant humiliation and the fabrication of a reason for the immediate turnaround. What a betrayal.

Meanwhile I was still pinned down on the bed. My knight in shining armor had lost all chivalry. I was still a virgin. The early Sixties mantra—"Why buy the cow, if you can get the milk for free?"—resounded from all maternal mouths. I just wanted out of the room. I begged to use his phone and told him I wanted to call my dad and a taxi.

Those words infuriated my "dream guy." He bit down on my left wrist. It hurt. It bled. It left an ugly bruise. He stomped out of the room and, five minutes later, deigned to let me use the phone. I don't remember what I said in my panicked call home. My dad said he would meet me at the terminal, and we would discuss the abrupt change of plans when I got home.

The airplane ride home turned nightmarish. There was an electrical storm, and lightning seemed to be coming through the window.

Extreme turbulence rocked the aircraft. It was a late night commuter flight, and landing at our destination airport became impossible due to snow. We were diverted to a neighboring facility. Dad had to change venues. By the time I connected with him, I was a wreck.

To hide the black and blue injury, I wore long sleeves for weeks. I never did explain the reason behind my frenzied return, claiming it was too painful to explain. I was too afraid of Dad's reaction. I was not very skilled in human nature – specifically man's nature. Would Dad fly up and confront Charming in person? My father's health was not the best. Mother told me he was eating and drinking too much. And his old back pain had resurfaced. Years earlier he had tilted backwards in a chair and fallen, and since then had to wear an uncomfortable brace. "Don't upset him," she warned.

Mother worried how she would explain my impromptu home-coming to the relatives. Dad never pressed the issue. I think he knew it had something to do with sex and decided to leave it at that.

Chapter 4

The final semester arrived. In mid-April, formal classes were canceled to enable us to study for comprehensive exams, highly mythologized for being roadblocks to even the most diligent student's graduation. The two weeks of preparation were torture, a prolonged worry, for two days of exams in French Literature, both oral and written to test my expertise in the field.

Success. I passed and would receive my diploma. Graduation loomed.

My parents arrived at the campus aglow. They had waited a long time for this auspicious day. The New England countryside was a perfect backdrop for the imminent prestigious ceremony. A renowned political speaker was reviewing his notes for the commencement address. My academic stress level finally dissolved. My French professor had just stopped my parents and me to compliment my final written analyses on Camus. A perfect day!

We heard a boisterous hello. It was my roommate's father and mother. My roommate and I—who had adjoining singles for the last two years—were polite and respectful of each other's mores. Because she had a fiancé she rarely stayed on campus on the weekends, Fridays included. She was planning a traditional Jewish wedding for Thanksgiving.

Her father patted my dad on the back in comradely fashion and declared we could all sit together. Dad blanched. He clenched his jaw. My parents had reached the culmination of their dream for me as a new member of the upper crust. Now it was going to be ruined; they didn't want to be associated with those of their ilk. I experienced a wave of nausea, and everything started spinning – vertigo brought on by my father's snobbery.

My heart was racing, my cheeks burning. I didn't want this kind family to feel put down. They were the Bronx, not Scarsdale, New York. So what? We were Brooklyn not the Hamptons.

"Please Dad, that sounds great," I said with fingers crossed.

He agreed. But one could feel the negative vibes.

Somehow I felt as if it were my fault, that I had chosen the wrong roommate.

I received my diploma. I had excelled intellectually, this tangible proof making me proud. Yet I didn't receive entry into elite society.

It was hard to return home to Brooklyn without a steady boy-friend. And without my own room.

When I was six, my parents had partitioned off part of their small bedroom with a cardboard-like panel to give me a fake chamber of my own, just a little more than the width of a twin bed. We had to place my dresser at the foot of the bed. The door to my quarters was only accessible by walking through my parents' bedroom. There was no lock. At twenty-one, this was far from acceptable; it offered less privacy than a single dorm room, no space to unwind from my parents' surveillance.

It was wearisome to be aware of how the other half lived, bathed in luxury. Sometimes ignorance is bliss! I felt so awkward back in the fold with Mother calling the shots. She reminded me constantly about the burden of paying back college loans. Since I didn't have a steady boyfriend or any prospects, it would be time to start thinking about a job.

The whole way through college my folks had hoped I would meet an eligible suitor, a bona fide Ivy Leaguer, and sweep him off his feet. Their expectations remained the same, but now they would be willing to compromise on the Ivy League status to accommodate the Brooklyn pool of bachelors. I, however, didn't have the chutzpah or self-confidence or voluptuousness to land an eligible catch.

Mother had gotten a long-term substitute position at a local public school, grade one. One day, three weeks after my return home, a colleague of Mom's, during a lunch conference in the teachers' room, suggested a blind date with her son, Barry. They lived nearby in affluent Manhattan Beach – in a single-story house, no less. One could walk over the pedestrian bridge from Sheepshead Bay and its apartment houses and commercial enterprises into this pocket of well-to-do community. I had always envied the people who lived in Manhattan Beach dwellings.

At the moment, Barry was between jobs, having just received his Accounting Degree from Syracuse University. I had been so betrayed by handsome, suave dates that I had decided to stay clear of them.

Mother said that Barry was quiet, introverted, and a really good son. She said nothing about his looks, save that he was tall. We were to meet the following night for a movie. At least it would get me out of the partition for several hours.

Who knew I would be married three weeks later?

Who knew what a nightmare my marriage would become?

Who knew what my reality would become?

Who knew?

And, more importantly, who would believe me?

When the doorbell rang, I walked slowly towards the sound. Blind dates fostered low expectations. It was the end of June, and I had other things on my mind. I was back to asking, "May I please have a dog?"

I sighed and opened the door. There he stood. Yes, he was tall, and trying ineffectively to appear casual. His smile was just a smidgen off. Barry wore a t-shirt and dungarees. His hair was curly, his nose a tad long. Eyeglasses completed the nerdy package. On a scale of one to ten (ten being a dreamboat) Barry was almost a six-and-a-half. I rated myself seven-and-a-half.

I could tell he was more than pleased with my appearance, as reflected in his look of relief. My pixie haircut, à la Audrey Hepburn, was growing out. Striking eyebrows, ordinary brown eyes framed by glasses. I had never forgotten the jeer, "No one makes passes at girls with glasses." I was glad Barry wore glasses too. I was taller than average, about twenty pounds overweight by my own strict calculations. The last semester at college had overflowed with pressure leading to excessive snacking.

When we came face to face, his shoulders relaxed, and his smile became more sincere.

After he sat down, the four of us endured a strained fifteen minutes of conventional small talk from weather to career choice. I noted that Barry cared little about impressing my parents; he seemed to get bored with the conversation and wasn't afraid to show it. At times, he didn't bother answering a question. I could see that my parents were less than enthused. Mother had spent all afternoon cleaning the apartment and choosing the menu. Dad had been warned by Mom to be cordial. Barry wouldn't play the deferential game obligatory to impressing the parents of a date. And that became glaringly exhibited at the table during the meal. The repast consisted of an elaborate hors d'oeuvres spread: gefilte fish, bagels and cream cheese, and potato pancakes with sour cream. Barry tended to slurp his food and chew quickly. He spoke with his mouth full. When Mother asked him to slow down, resentment flickered across his face. And he didn't. Slow down, that is.

By the time we left to go to the show, I knew that my parents didn't like him. At all. He didn't meet their standard of eligibility; he was a college grad with some money, but not even close to having class.

I shared some of their negativity, but I could accept a little gaucheness at the dinner table. There are worse things. It wasn't like he didn't use a fork and knife. I couldn't imagine he was being ill-mannered by design.

After the painful dining experience, we walked out the door to the elevator. Barry turned to me. "I don't think your parents like me. That's okay. I don't care for them either.

It doesn't matter, as long as you like me."

"Well, I wish you would try to be more friendly with my folks," I responded.

"I don't humor people. I am who I am."

I wasn't thrilled but felt that I could deal with this flaw. My parents were very hard to please.

"Barry, I don't want any battles with my parents, just a truce. I'd really appreciate it if you would at least be civil."

"In that case, maybe."

I don't recall the movie. I was too absorbed in how Barry was trying to get the nerve to put his arm around me in the darkened theater. Hesitant is good, I thought.

On the way home, Barry told me about his boat – a rowboat with an outboard motor. The promise of a ride on the bay was enticing. I hoped to make this relationship work.

He didn't try to kiss me goodnight.

The truth was Barry arrived at the right time in my life. He had a B.S. degree and came from an affluent background. My exaggerated notions of true love had dissolved after my college dating fiascos. Geeky was better than suave. And Barry was Jewish. He would relieve the stress of feeling inferior in social class. I agreed with the maxim that Jewish men made the best fathers. I had heard it all my life. It was becoming important for me to build a family that I could nurture with warmth and affection, a family with unconditional love. I could almost taste independence. My life would have to change. The only solution I could see was marriage.

Barry's family was more supportive than my parents. His mother, who had arranged the blind date, was happy we were seeing each other. She doted on her youngest son. Barry's older brother lived out of town with his wife and two kids. His father kept to himself and was totally absorbed in his successful garment business. He was dominated by his wife as demonstrated by screaming matches about important issues like the price of canned tuna at the local market. They seemed pleased, even relieved, that Barry had found a potential wife.

The following week, my folks were going on a trip to the

Adirondacks in Upper State New York. Because I was dating someone so close by, it wasn't considered proper for me to stay home alone. They thought people would talk. So if I wanted to remain in the city, I had to stay with my aunt, my dad's sister, who lived on Long Island about an hour's drive away.

After a week of commuting back and forth – a quick courtship consisting of beach days, picnics, movies, and dancing "The Twist" – Barry and I decided to elope. This meant I could skirt around my parents' derogatory feelings about Barry and announce the nuptials to them later, when it was a done deal. Besides, I couldn't visualize my father walking me down the aisle with Barry as groom. My dad disliked Barry so much; he found him unbearably rude. So I took it upon myself to get it done quickly, so I wouldn't have to ask them for permission or pay for part of an unwelcome wedding. I was not rebelling against my parents but avoiding an impossible situation. I thought they might not have even wanted to attend.

It should be no surprise that Barry and I hadn't really discussed anything of an intense nature, like our values or habits – whether we were even compatible. We didn't talk about dreams, desires, or children. Or even a honeymoon. We only discussed the immediate decision to wed. I wanted my own space away from my parents. Barry had his own agenda; he wanted to snap off my bra (a euphemism for sex). Sexual intimacy was permitted only in marriage, or so I thought. In a rash moment of distorted enthusiasm, we agreed to get married. We were pragmatic, not passionate.

I wasn't giving up on a long-held fantasy. I had never dreamed about a fairy tale wedding, or actually any wedding at all. I had never played with Barbie dolls. I didn't care about an engagement ring. I had only one goal.

We arrived at the Brooklyn courthouse chamber of the justice of the peace. All the necessary papers were in order. Barry brought a friend and his fiancée to be witnesses of our civil ceremony. I wore an orange summer shift, Barry a sports jacket and slacks. We were seated in a waiting room with five other couples when we heard our names called in a perfunctory manner.

Romantic? Not particularly. I felt more guilty than excited, petrified of my parents' reaction when they found out that their perfect daughter had eloped. As it sunk in that I was really going through with this marriage, I started to panic. My thoughts were permeated by the obligatory phone call to my aunt, after the ceremony, explaining why I wouldn't be back that night. And then I realized I had overlooked yet another major faux pas: my parents wouldn't be the first to know I had gotten married. Mother would be furious I had not told her first and that she received the news second hand.

The ceremony was hurried, unemotional. We had not taken the time to write our own vows.

After we became husband and wife, it was time to dial my aunt.

"Hello," I mumbled shakily.

"What's wrong? Why are you calling? You sound strange."

"You'll never guess. I just got married!" I tried to sound enthusiastic, but it came out as incredulity.

"I didn't even know you were seriously dating someone. Do your folks know?"

"No, you're the only one."

"Your parents are going to be devastated. They'll feel betrayed. Who is this guy?"

"His name is Barry. I won't be back for a few days. Please call my parents and tell them about the marriage. They're at Lake Inn in

Saranac. Thank you. I love you."

I hung up quickly before she could say anything else. I didn't want concrete feedback. In my heart, I knew that this elopement was the lesser of two evils. My worries about getting married so hastily were overshadowed by my wish to escape never-ending criticism from my parents. I did feel remiss that I'd given this onerous task to my sweet aunt. I just couldn't face my parents' wrath. I had managed to postpone the inevitable fallout, even if only for a short while.

Barry called his mother. She wished us luck and looked forward to our return.

Barry and I decided on a honeymoon destination: the Motel on the Terrace about an hour's drive to New Jersey. Looking back, I can't believe my lack of expectations: I never planned for an exotic getaway, I just wanted to be married. Maybe I felt I didn't deserve bridal extravagances. Or maybe deep down I felt my act of defiance did not warrant a champagne celebration.

We indulged in a grandiose dinner at Lindy's, one of New York's popular restaurants, known for its famous cheesecake. My parents would have loved it. I overindulged out of nervousness. We then bought wine and Triscuits for the motel room.

Tomes have been written about splendiferous wedding nights, the culmination of joy and fulfillment. I, like many others, had been indoctrinated into the notion that marriage was the ultimate moment of togetherness. In the early sixties, many brides were virgins. Living together first was rare, or so I perceived. Now I would no longer have to be the third wheel at a motel vacation my parents and I took annually as a family.

We left the restaurant. The car ride up the curving road was making me dizzy. I tried to will away the discomfort, to no avail. I was struck by nausea and a pounding headache. A really bad headache. Too much food, too much wine, and, of course, too much guilt.

We arrived at the motel. I just wanted to lie down and concentrate on not vomiting in front of my new husband. I looked around at the ordinary accommodations, nothing special. What about the luxurious lodging in the brochure? *What have I done?* I wondered.

Barry was busy checking out the room. "Barry, may we talk for a minute?" I uttered as he placed our bags on a rack. I wanted him to know that I needed some time to try to recover my equilibrium. "A couple of aspirin and a half hour of rest should make me feel better. Could you get me a glass of water?"

Instead of water he brought me champagne and a platter of Triscuits, wanting to toast our future. The few sips I took sent me over the edge, and I was horrified at the thought I was about to throw up. (To this day, I glare at Triscuits on the grocery shelves and remember. Remember the hurt.)

"Barry, may we talk for a minute?"

I could see by the expression on his face that he didn't want to talk. He responded by ignominiously pushing me down on the bed, beginning to undress me, fumbling with buttons in his haste.

"Please stop," I asked. "Let's wait a minute – I really feel sick. I'm not kidding."

"Don't be a tease. I don't accept silly, weak excuses. At any time!"

A tease? Was he kidding? Teasing takes gumption. I had always been so submissive when it came to my mother and father, I would never have been brave enough to try being manipulative.

Where had my nerdy, safe boyfriend gone? I became frightened at this unexpected rough handling and shocking words.

Once again an authoritarian was telling me what to do. Not

asking, but demanding. I reacted in my usual pattern, yielding. And thus, I painfully lost my virginity with tears running down my cheeks, my head pounding, trying hard not to throw up.

He penetrated me three more times that night. It seemed strange to me that tears didn't deter him. I thought his lack of consideration might have been due to having had too much to drink. Maybe his thinking and his actions were impaired. Maybe it was just an alcoholic mishap.

I woke up early next morning determined to recapture a semblance of romance. I tried to slip to the bathroom; my bladder was bursting. As soon as I moved, he initiated sex. I later learned to avoid stirring in bed whenever possible.

Was this what marriage meant? I asked my inexperienced self. *Sex multiple times a day, ready or not?* In my short years, I had no basis for comparison. What about all those "I've got a headache" cartoons, where the wife uses that excuse and receives a pass? What about "Moon River" and the rainbow's end?

The rest of the vacation made up for his untempered bedroom behavior. For all I knew about sex mores, maybe it was only I who felt Barry's actions were excessive. We swam in the pool, hiked and biked on the mountain trails. We dined. Everything was normal except I had to learn to submit to his obsessive sexual demands.

One night we had gone to the movies in town after dinner. *Lawrence of Arabia,* I think. We arrived back at the motel late. I was tired but wouldn't admit it. I didn't want him to become upset at me, accusing me of trying to get out of sex.

Casually I grabbed a handful of Triscuits since I had passed on the popcorn, and we sat talking about the movie. Then he told me it was time for bed. I noticed a slight change from the earlier aggressiveness;

he seemed preoccupied.

"Anything wrong?" I asked him. I was relieved. But curious.

"I don't like using condoms. It cuts down on my sensation. I want to stop using them."

He wanted to start using double protection, which meant my using spermicidal foam and a diaphragm.

"We can't risk having babies."

What did he mean, no babies? Now, or never? I didn't ask. Somehow it sounded like never.

We were going home in three days to Barry's parents' house, a temporary stop before looking for our own apartment. Immediately he set up a doctor's appointment for a diaphragm fitting. I couldn't believe his irrational alacrity. Children, whom I could love unconditionally, were a major priority for getting married. For a moment I thought about running back to my parents' home since I wanted children so badly. But then I deluded myself into thinking I could change his mind. Many young brides subscribed to the theory of transformation. If he desired me so much, he would want me to be happy. After all, marriage meant progeny. Didn't it?

I was very tense at the gynecologist's. I had never had a pelvic exam before and was embarrassed as the male doctor examined me. I had never even heard of a diaphragm. Afraid to anger Barry, I just hoped I understood the contraceptive instructions. I returned home non-triumphantly with my package.

Barry and I rented a converted basement studio near both our parents, cheap but in Manhattan Beach. Our apartment was really just one large room divided into sections. A screen separated the tiny kitchen and designated bedroom. Another area featured a sofa and

TV. The landlady, who lived upstairs, kept her washer and dryer smack in the corner of our "living room." She reserved the right to use her appliances anytime at her convenience, retaining a key to the basement for that purpose. It sounded fair to me. We didn't have visitors because both sets of parents felt we didn't belong renting someone's basement. In fact, it was the only thing on which they agreed.

I longed for Mom and Dad's acceptance. I had not yet given up on reconciliation. My parents never really recovered from my elopement. They had gone from furious to hurt to a state of parental martyrdom. They had not forgiven me. They did nothing to mask their disappointment. Barry was all too aware of their attitude. He didn't care.

My mild CPA husband wasn't only interested in numbers. Our social isolation gave Barry license to purchase special reading material for the coffee table. Magazines called *Sexology* and pornography from Sweden. Pictures I never knew existed, let alone were available to buy. We're not talking mild *Playboy* here. Women in chains being raped. Tangles of men and women, naked, genitalia everywhere. Multiple postures. I was appalled and saddened by the pictures depicting bestiality. Turned on, Barry said I had to peruse the garish periodicals with him. I longed for sensitivity, not pictorial jolts.

So began my introduction to a darker interpretation of sex. Ménages à trois, bondage, masturbation, orgies, Marquis de Sade. Crass. I couldn't believe it. He wanted to share these photos. Every day. Multiple times. He forbade me to lock the bathroom door. He even wanted to hold my hand when he was on the toilet as a turn-on.

As the days progressed, our landlady became annoyed. She couldn't get her laundry done. We were always in bed. She would knock on the door at the top of the staircase and say, "It's time for me to do my wash."

Barry would answer, "It's not a good time."

When she came back a couple hours later, the scenario remained the same. She asked if we ever got out of bed. Or she would shout, "This is sick! I need clean clothes! Are you a nymphomaniac?"

After I looked up "nymphomaniac," I was totally rattled and embarrassed. Barry's hyper-sexuality was reaching the public. I didn't know what to say. I stayed silent. Barry thought it was funny. This was not a newlywed romp. This was a marathon sexual encounter fueled by pornography. I had been doubting my own sanity as regards to sexual mores. This had been uncharted territory, outside my knowledge. The landlady validated my thoughts through the door. So it was true. His sexual demands were excessive.

It took me a long time to realize that what I thought was unbridled desire was really a lust for power. Complete control over another person can become a heady obsession.

We were asked to leave the apartment by the end of the month. We were evicted for blocking laundry. We had only signed a month to month agreement which included the landlady's ongoing washer and dryer rights. Fortunately, Barry was offered an entry-level job as an accountant in New Jersey so we had to move anyway. We found a small apartment near his work with coin-operated washing machines on the lower level for all tenants.

It was the middle of August so I had time to register at the school districts as a first year teacher. I had new status as a Mrs., which meant that I had a valid place in society. I was a bona fide adult, and Barry looked good on paper. It bolstered my self-confidence; having a husband proved I was a capable grownup, no longer my parents' pawn. In a way, I felt I had arrived in the world. I had my own family. I had failed at the prom, the pinning, the engagement. But now I had achieved the goal of belonging to the majority.

There was an opening for a ninth grade French longtime substitute. I jumped at the chance to embrace my new status and lose myself in a career.

On one of my first days of school, I looked so young that a monitor sent me to the principal's office for talking in the hall, much to the amusement of my students. The next week, a parent said I looked too juvenile to wear lipstick, let alone be the instructor.

My confidence blossomed. I enjoyed my days immensely. Teaching was more than a job; it was a calling. My sensitivity became an asset instead of a liability because I appreciated my students' individuality. I never forced a shy student to give a speech, nor did I give up on a student who couldn't master the assignment. I watched like a hawk for peer ridicule when it came to French pronunciation, known to daunt many a student. Self-worth was fostered in the classroom in addition to academic expertise. I felt things were finally working out in the professional arena.

But then the sword of Damocles fell.

Some people, like Barry, think that teachers have an easy job. They think we leave work early, have holidays off, and enjoy a free all-summer vacation. The truth is we have a mountain of papers to grade. Lessons to plan. Phone calls to return. At least two hours each school night and part of the weekend.

I had just cleaned up the kitchen after dinner and was sitting at the table with a formidable stack of quizzes to grade when I heard

Barry stomping around.

"All right. This has got to stop," he blustered, marching into the room.

"What are you talking about?" I asked, startled.

"You can't bring your schoolwork home to do at night anymore. I won't allow it!"

"Excuse me?"

"You heard me. I want your attention in the evening."

"It's part of my job. I don't have a choice."

"Then you have to make it up to me."

My heart fell. Now he was interfering with my standards of con-scientious grading. This did not bode well for my murky marriage.

To make the marriage more tolerable, I began to beg Barry for a pet. I had to make a sexual deal. There was a pattern forming here. I was permitted (and I earned it in the bedroom) to have a parakeet. For every new favor granted, I always had to "make it up to him." I taught myself to block him out during sex. To think of what I wanted and forget the pathway.

My parents picked up on my unhappiness when they called daily to say hello. They had somewhat mellowed towards me. They knew, or suspected, that the awkward, rather bumbling façade that Barry presented to the public masked an unkind, controlling individual with an exaggerated sense of entitlement. But I couldn't verify that to Mom and Dad. They heard undercurrents in my voice and in my hesitations about my new daily routine. My folks encouraged me to leave him. They had forgiven me for the elopement and were now focused on a divorce. I didn't listen. Teaching and preparation absorbed most of my time. I was too busy for a major change.

One Wednesday evening, Barry was being particularly demanding. I had exams to prepare and had settled at the kitchen table with my textbooks. He came in with that look in his eye, and I prayed I was mistaken. I hoped he just wanted a snack. I held my breath, didn't move.

He took a can of beer out of the refrigerator and slammed the door shut. He grabbed a bag of chips from the pantry.

"Come on, Wife," he ordered.

I pretended that I didn't hear.

"I'm speaking to you," he continued.

"I have some work to do before the morning. I'll be there in about forty-five minutes."

"You'll come now!" I heard from behind me. "Feel this." He thrust his erect penis against my neck, leaning over my papers, scattering some to the floor. A few ripped as he stepped on the assignments. Barry pulled me up and yanked me to the bedroom.

I was resigned and waited for it to be over. Yet my body started to respond. His Sexology magazines had taught him the magic spots. He concentrated on my clitoris. I had an orgasm.

He laughed, a mean, ridiculing laugh.

"Now, isn't that better than working? I knew you'd get with the program."

I realized that I had to take my parakeet and clear out of our apartment. I couldn't stand it anymore. I chose to survive the I-told-you-so's from my parents, rather than live as sexual chattel.

I readied my clothes, books, and my bird, Billie. Two days later, while Barry was at work, my parents arrived to help me move into a motel near my school. One of their friends was a lawyer, and he was to assist with the divorce.

Mother and Dad were delighted to gloat over my failure. Dad was doing better financially, and Mother would have another chance to pick an "appropriate" man for me. They had waited for this moment from the day they heard I had married Barry. They never asked what prompted my decision to leave; they just assumed that I had finally come to my senses. Besides, I could never tell them about my problems in bed. Sex and the body were strictly private matters, not to be discussed, ever.

Two weeks passed, and I had not heard from Barry. It felt strange living in a room off the highway. I had never been alone in such an environment before. At first I had tried to think of it as an adventure – complimentary continental breakfast, maid service, private TV. My parakeet, Billie, kept happily chirping in the new surroundings, especially when the sun bounced off the window. There even was a nook for studying.

But I started getting nervous. The noise of the passing cars was downright spooky. I had unwanted visions of someone breaking into the room. How many people had keys to my door? Could they be trusted? I relaxed when my parents or my lawyer came to visit for an hour or so. In the evening, returning from the adjacent coffee shop alone, I felt lucky that Billie was waiting to welcome me. I covered his cage as late as possible every night.

It was almost Thanksgiving when I started feeling ill. Nauseated all day, I thought I had caught the flu from my students. I dismissed a passing thought: I knew I couldn't be pregnant because we consistently used double protection.

Oh, but I was…

It was the early sixties. Contraception was not yet perfected.

I didn't know what to do. I had always dreamed of having children. I had promised myself that I would dote on a baby. Babies needed two parents, and my marriage was on the verge of extinction.

After receiving the positive results from the doctor's office (no home pregnancy tests at the time) I tried to sort through the news. My thoughts were a jumble: a dream come true? Barry's furious reaction? Mother's certain-to-be hysteria? Random, mundane issues tumbled through my mind—grades due, bird treats to buy—meshed with the serious focal point of what to do.

Following a week of indecision, and the onset of severe morning sickness, interspersed with lesson plans on French conjugation and idiomatic phrases, I knew once again that it was time for a formidable phone call. No more procrastination. I was worn out.

I started to dial and hung up. *Grow up*, I admonished myself.

I dialed again and hung up on the first ring.

"This is so immature," I told Billie, who was watching me sideways through his cage.

"Hello," Billie responded. It was one of the handful of words he had recently mastered. I took the hint.

The third time I dialed, I didn't hang up. "Hello, Mom."

"How are you doing? Have you signed any papers yet?"

"About that," I hesitated. "I have something to tell you."

"Uh-oh. I don't like the sound of that."

"Listen, Mother. I'm about eight weeks pregnant." I held my

breath, didn't hear any response. "Mother, are you still there?"

I got an earful, punctuated intermittently with, "Wait till your father finds out!"

The gist of her tirade was that I couldn't be tied to Barry. It would ruin my life. Then she totally shocked me, saying I had to have an abortion. She would pay for me to go to Mexico at a reputable clinic. It was the only answer. Immediately, thoughts of hangers, back alleys, and infection crossed my mind. I was horrified at the thought of dismissing my dream of becoming a mother. I, who tried to save a sick puppy from a pet shop ... I, who rushed to help a wounded bird and had never said "no" to Mom before ... I felt faint. This time I knew I had no choice but to defy her. Abortion? Not an option.

After my mother's rant, I knew returning to my parents' home was not feasible. Returning to Barry was, if he would take me back. There was a good chance that he would: Barry had found out where I was staying by following me home from school one day. He had called to tell me he would always love me and asked me to please come back. He said we could work things out.

When I told him I was pregnant, over the phone, he promised to accept the baby.

I returned to our apartment with renewed hope that things would improve.

Meanwhile Mother kept phoning, urging me to just leave him. She had accepted the pregnancy but stepped up her anti-Barry campaign. Her dislike of him had escalated after I had shared some nuggets of information about Barry: that he really had no friends and that he monopolized my time, interfering with my job.

Barry started fuming at these daily calls because I got so upset afterwards. I wanted to mend fences with Mother so she could fulfill the role of grandma. I should have stopped taking her phone calls. But I was hoping for peace, for some measure of acceptance. After one of these conversations, I started spotting. My ob/gyn advised me to avoid Mother for the duration of the pregnancy or I might miscarry. The emotional turmoil might be too much.

Barry was of little help at this time. Even though he said that he would accept the baby,

he didn't want his sexual routine changed. Barry felt that intercourse was natural and not harmful at this time. He called my fear of spotting again "childish." He chose to ignore any restrictions on his desires. I was miserable and frightened.

Two months after my return, Barry's CPA firm opened a branch in California, and we decided to move. He hadn't been getting along with his colleagues. His questionable mannerisms and mean-spirited sarcasm were not appealing to management. I hated leaving my job, but the thought of raising a baby in a new state seemed serendipitous.

Dad was enthusiastic about the move. He said he had always wanted me to see other parts of the country, to expand my life experience. His participation in the European Theater during WWII had left him with a sense of curiosity about the world. He felt that moving from the East to the West Coast would be good for me. Or so he stated. Or maybe he was relieved to have my imperfect, impolite husband far away. Would missing me be collateral damage? Mother was conflicted, thinking the relatives would find it strange for an only daughter to want to be so far away. But clearly Barry being out of sight was a plus.

The plane trip wasn't pleasant. I had never liked flying. I kept trying to read, to soothe the parakeet under the seat, and to enjoy the baby kicking. I brushed Barry's hand off my thigh. Maybe this could be a new beginning.

California was not Brooklyn. We stayed at a motel on El Camino Road in Mountain View until we rented a duplex. It had a small yard, two bedrooms, in a rural area. There were no sidewalks but lots of gravel. Our only neighbors were two working adults, so it was quiet during the day. Fine with me.

I connected immediately with an ob-gyn and concentrated on all things baby. The new firm offered health benefits, and Barry's co-workers suggested a small, private group. I had no experience at all with infants or their care. Choices had to be made. A diaper service? A cradle or crib? Breast-feeding or formula? Suddenly, Barry was interested. I was leaning towards breast-feeding when Barry gave his opinion.

"I think you should definitely breast-feed," he suggested.

I couldn't believe he was participating in this decision. He wasn't looking forward to the birth – especially the twelve-week hiatus for sex. He told me I would have to "make it up to him." How I came to deplore those words.

"Why?" I naively queried about his reaction to my dilemma about nourishment.

"It's a done deal."

"Why?" I repeated.

"So I won't have to buy milk anymore. You can nurse me too."

I examined his expression to see if he were kidding. He wasn't.

I selected Similac, the powdered infant formula.

Chapter 5

The contractions were strong and coming frequently. I wanted to go to the hospital right away. I was scared. I had not taken any birthing courses. I didn't know what to expect. Barry was focused on taking pictures of me making a phone call to the obstetrician in my nightgown.

My doctor was not overly concerned because it was the first baby, and labor was usually extended. But he understood my history of lacking familial support and preference to be in a positive environment. He said to come to the hospital immediately.

The drive to the hospital was silent. No kind words. No encouragement. Just silence.

In the hospital, the contractions abated; the pain, however, did not. When I was given a sedative known as "twilight sleep," typical at that time for prolonged births, Barry went home for a good night's rest. After twenty-one hours, I finally gave birth. A seven pound boy!

Barry expressed neither elation nor distress. As soon as we got home, he began the six week countdown to permitted sexual intercourse. I was not surprised at his priority.

Inundated with love, I was ecstatic about the baby, Michael. I wanted to stop every pedestrian on the street to shout, "I have a son!" For the first time in my life, I felt true unabridged joy.

My parents sent me money for a baby nurse. I really appreciated it. For two whole weeks. Barry didn't feel that I needed help yet I had no experience at all with infants, from changing diapers, to burping, to supporting the head properly. My parents were planning to visit in three months. Nevertheless, I knew that I could handle anything or anyone now – I had a son.

I loved the infant routine: bottles, diapers, naps, and baths. Motherhood became my cherished calling, each day a stepping stone to a burgeoning confidence. My weekdays were incredibly wonderful – and Barry was at work.

My obligatory concession to make up for the lack of intimacy, even though it was a medical necessity, had been twelve weeks of masturbating Barry twice a day to that end. I pretended my hand was a mechanical device. At least I never had to kiss him. His kisses were devoid of affection, a combination of anger and lust. For me, sex was a chore, not unlike scrubbing the bathtub and shower stall or washing the dishes. Barry didn't mind my kissing abstinence. It was all about him.

When the six-week end of self-restraining arrived, I was ordered to hire our baby nurse for a night out with Barry to celebrate. It would be my first time away from baby Michael since he was born. Barry laughed at my separation anxiety and forbade me to think about anyone but him. At the restaurant he embarrassed me by putting his hands suggestively over my shoulders, to the extent that some of the neighboring diners *tss*ked.

I knew there was a pay phone outside the ladies' room. I wanted to call home to check on Michael, but Barry told me if I got up, we'd go straight home to bed. I dared not move. On top of everything I was afraid intercourse would be painful after childbirth. Obviously I couldn't share these fears with Barry. I sat and moved the food around on my plate and watched him scarf down his dinner.

When we returned to baby, Michael was sleeping peacefully. I thanked the nurse, and Barry paid her.

The door closed, and my husband led me into the bedroom.

And now the fine-tuned sexual repression of my life began. When I looked into Barry's eyes while he was pounding away in me, I saw wrath, domination, and a creepy sort of rapacity. I knew I had to do something for my own well-being.

I chose to surround myself with things that I loved. I still wanted a dog. After listening to me beg for months, Barry had an idea. A Polaroid camera. If I wanted a puppy, I'd have to make sex photos for him.

This was the first time he wanted to make me an actual part of his pornography collection. I didn't feel comfortable knowing that there would be visual proof of my being a party to kinkiness.

But in the end I agreed. I thought I would feel uncomfortable in the moment, but that the photos would be rather innocuous. I'd just block them out. I could get a Labrador puppy, and maybe Barry would leave me alone for a while. He could jerk off at his leisure looking at the pictures. I had heard somewhere that new brides should be able to manipulate their husbands with sex, but in my case, it was the opposite. My husband used his addiction to sexual gratification as an all-encompassing bargaining chip. He bought me a special wardrobe, items I designated "sperm dresses." He would look at my photos and ejaculate on these black clothes. He insisted on keeping them in his closet. Unwashed.

Barry even bought one of those life-sized, anatomically correct rubber dolls. I worried that when my parents would visit, somehow they would discover the play things in his closet.

Sometimes, when I couldn't stand being in front of the camera anymore, I would cry. He took the pictures anyway, at times using a tripod to film himself too. He had set up his own dark room to develop the photos. Obviously he couldn't bring them to the local photo drive-up or twenty-four-hour pharmacy.

I was living a double life. Mother during the day, sex toy by night. Make-believe young, dedicated homemaker masking a lost, floundering individual.

Meanwhile Barry wasn't really interested in Michael. He never picked him up or played with him one-on-one for the sheer fun of it. At that time, fathers weren't so involved with their babies' care. But Barry took this practice to a whole new level. He wasn't emotionally engaged. Michael was a tangent in his sacrosanct, narcissistic routine.

However, Baby was my little prince. I gloried in Michael's monthly progress. He was an easy baby. At eight months, he raced around the house in his walker, chased the puppy, and smiled at the parakeet. Life was better, but I still worried about my pictures. I brushed the concerns aside. *Everyone has something to hide.*

Soon the desire for another baby kicked in; the coveted sibling gap of two years inundated my mind. Memories of my lonely child-hood superseded the reality of my cloudy situation. I could not find the energy to leave Barry and start again. Like the adage states, one stays with the unhappiness one lives with and knows, in lieu of chancing the unhappiness of an unknown. I was getting used to numbing my body and using sex for allowance, perks, and even permission to answer the doorbell. Yes, the doorbell. If my parents were at the door coming for a visit, he would drag me into the bathroom for a quickie. I didn't want to cry because my dad would pick up on the tears and ask me what was wrong. So I endured stoically, without emotion. Then I was permitted to open the front door.

I knew in my heart that I shouldn't have to put up with such domination. And now any respite at my parents' was negated by three thousand miles. Yet to have another baby was a riveting primal instinct. I wanted Michael to have a sibling. I wondered what it would cost me...

I found out. The photography was pushed up a notch. To movies. This was the deal. I could have another baby if I made a sex movie. A long one. Since I was no longer a novice in sexual barter, I thought I could handle it. The photography had become more boring than outlandish.

"I really want another woman to join us," Barry whined.

That request had become old hat. I would call his bluff. "Fine. But you have to find her and get her to agree." I knew that he wouldn't accept that stipulation. He was only a macho, dominant male when it came to me.

"Forget it for now. It'll be the two of us."

Barry set up the tripod and locked the door.

What possessed me to stay with this man? Convenience? His affluent background? Or my feeling that I couldn't attract another man, especially now, wanting another baby? I abandoned my quest to find "true" love.

Over and over, I played Roberta Flack's "The First Time Ever I Saw Your Face." Glen Campbell was another favorite, "By the Time I Get to Phoenix." I read *The Fountainhead* and other novels during the day with the music in the background. Needless to say, bedtime reading had to be duly negotiated.

I had my second son, Carl, a year later. With two young children to take care of, I was beyond busy. Meanwhile my husband was mastering the art of control. One day when he forced me to go to White Front to look for hardware with him, he literally dragged me around the aisles and verbally ridiculed me for wanting to go home. Carl started to cry. Michael was scared of Barry's raised voice calling his mother "an emotional baby."

At my next pediatric appointment, a few weeks afterward, the doctor told me he had seen me at White Front. I felt myself blushing. I was mortified.

"Why do you put up with your husband's actions? He's so nasty."

"I don't have enough money to leave."

"But you don't deserve that treatment," he continued.

How could I tell this kind, Jewish doctor why I was stuck in this relationship? It was too complicated. I hardly understood myself.

I tried not to respond to Barry's constant "lovemaking." Affection, aka cuddling, was nonexistent. He started calling me a "frigid log." Unceasingly. At times my body still would betray me, and I would reach an orgasm in spite of myself. Upon which I would hear his ridiculing snicker. Thank goodness I didn't have to kiss him, which forever became more intimate to me than any act of intercourse.

At least my boys were too young to understand. They didn't realize that other children could jump in their parents' beds in the morning to snuggle. Barry never threw them in the air to hear giggles. On weekends, he stayed in the master bedroom, a martyr because he had to work all week. We never went on family outings unless Barry felt there was something in it for his personal enjoyment, like flying his remote control plane.

Chapter 6

I had never felt like a pretty twenty-something. I felt unattractive and worn-out. My ego had not remained unscathed by constant marital put downs. My demeaning sex life had me wondering if I could ever enjoy myself in bed. Or was Barry the norm?

Daily routine continued. When I failed a vision test and was given a stronger prescription, I chose new eyeglasses with cute frames. There was a half-off sale. Michael and Carl accompanied me – one in a stroller with Cheerios spread on his tray, the other armed with coloring books and crayons. I was taken aback when during the frame and lens measurement, the optician's knees pressed against mine under the table.

I thought I was imagining things. The man was handsome and athletic. A hunk. And, I later found out, a tennis whiz. When his hand touched my thigh – rather gently, not in a crass way – I considered it a gesture of caring, perhaps even friendliness. I started shaking, thinking I was out of my league with someone so dashing. I blushed. My hands became clammy. I was astounded that someone was making a pass at me. For all my married experience, I was extremely naïve about the pleasures of sex. I wanted to know if there were men who were kind in the bedroom. Someone just can't take all that abuse without wonder. Was sex a continual power display? Or could it be something else?

I checked to see if he were wearing a wedding band. Yes! He was safe. He had a wife and later, I found out, two children. Even better. To me that meant I could trust him. Even if we flirted a little, he wouldn't want to risk his own marital situation. I knew he wouldn't call Barry and betray me because I could always reciprocate and call his wife. All this whimsy amidst the commonplace.

My glasses would be ready in two weeks. If he were interested in seeing me, would I consider it? I was hesitant but starved for affection. Was I really frigid? Was I only attractive in sperm dresses?

Who had I become? Truly, I was shy. Perhaps I wanted one tryst, to hold on to a romantic memory. A script change. I had been fitted with an IUD, so I was being responsible. Barry had insisted on this device, refusing to acknowledge the possibility of negative side effects. My varicose veins prevented me from using the Pill, so the IUD was the next best protection.

When pick-up day arrived, the optician sat down at the table with lollipops. For all of us, Michael, Carl, and me, the green one mine. This simple gesture melted my heart. I was starved for affection.

As he adjusted the frames on my face, he leaned over and whispered, "Could we meet at lunchtime soon?"

Impulsively, I nodded in the affirmative, too nonplussed to speak.

We arranged to meet in two days.

During those waiting days I fantasized constantly about the appointment. I played Frank Sinatra's "My Way" repeatedly. Vacillating about my decision, I arranged for a congenial neighbor to babysit swap for one and a half hours. Our children had played together before, and my boys always looked forward to using someone else's toys. When they heard they were going, they had no qualms about my leaving for a little while. In that short space of time, I would try to appear sophisticated and cool. I'd perform an Oscar-winning role in my fairy tale script and hope for rave reviews. I was determined that my likely lover wouldn't know that I had no experience and had slept with only one man. And that that man had showed me only the ignoble side of so-called love-making.

I reached some sort of plateau of being humiliated and blackmailed in the bedroom. Barry started threatening to show my sex pictures to my father. My dad would have gone ballistic. A heart attack was a possibility. With the fear of my dad's health, I had to acquiesce more often. It was becoming more and more intolerable. I thought of Barry's manipulative coercion, and with it, an awakening desire for revenge. I would get vindication, even if I were the only one to know about it.

When the day arrived, I was in emotional turmoil. It felt like make-believe suddenly turned into reality. If one of my children fell sick, if my car wouldn't start, or if Barry took a personal day, then my plans would not come to fruition. I dared not eat breakfast, my stomach was too upset. My left eye twitched from stress. My hands were cold as ice. I didn't know what to wear. All the planning had been enervating, and I just wanted it to be over without getting caught. I couldn't imagine the consequences if Barry found out. Could I pull off this alter-ego, feigning to be a sexually liberated, no-strings-attached woman? It was the late sixties, and somewhere out there was a hippie sexual revolution. Maybe this was my subtle participation in the new sexual freedom.

In spite of my misgivings, I was carried along by the momentum of the fantasy text. I had expended too much effort to stop now. Besides, who knew when another opportunity for a rendezvous would come along? I wanted this dream to hold onto. More than anything, I desired a memory of the tryst.

Later that morning my savvy neighbor wished me luck. I mumbled "thanks" and left shakily for the car. The encounter was set for a parking lot, two towns over. We'd go to a motel together in one car and stay for an hour.

I was inexorably on the way. Stop, go, right turn, first left. I toyed with turning around. This guy towards whom I was driving was a soft-spoken, handsome, magnetic stranger. Truly an unknown. My resolve stabilized. Okay, I could do this.

We met in front of the designated supermarket, parking two rows away from each other. My heart raced. I was acutely aware of the humdrum of shopping carts and automated doors. I felt calmer when he took my hand.

The motel across the way took on a beckoning glow. Usually, motels signified boredom and Barry. This one projected glamor: wisteria over the portals, a koi pond, rattan patio furniture. The fact that I knew nothing about this man made the date more alluring. Still I felt compelled to hide behind a potted palm when he checked us in at the registration desk as Mr. and Mrs.

Room 107 was on the ground floor facing the rear driveway. When he opened the door, I hesitantly followed him in, feeling bashful.

I stood still. Moving around me, he closed the door, sat on the double bed equipped with "Magic Fingers," and motioned for me to join him.

I was still immobile, but the attraction was strong. We had already used up twenty minutes, including the travel time. I didn't have the time to waver. Taking a deep breath, I sat down next to him. He kissed me gently, his lips smooth and soft. I couldn't believe the sensations. As he undressed me, I realized that I would always consider this moment my actual wedding night.

I experienced my first orgasm not fraught with scorn. I never knew there were so many erotic spots on the body and couldn't believe it was I who moaned. At this moment, I forgot my other concerns except that of having my lover enter me. Absorb the wetness. Stop the throbbing. Desire had usurped chafing and discomfit. When I looked up at his face, I did not see Barry's strange look of domination.

And the *pièce de résistance*: I was told to look under the pillow. I pulled out a sample size box of Godiva chocolates. I, who had taught myself not to cry, began tearing up. (Crying intensified Barry's arousal. When I didn't want to have sex or pictures taken, I would plead for him to stop. If I started to sob, it turned him on even more. The sex lasted longer and became more abusive. He didn't care that I was sore. I focused on how much I resented him, not tears.)

So I wasn't frigid. I lay in my lover's arms for the few minutes we had left.

"Thank you for everything." I snuggled close to him.

"My pleasure."

Out of nowhere I asked him, "What is your favorite song?"

"'Mrs. Robinson,' from *The Graduate*. Why?"

"I'm going to buy the record and relive our lovemaking when I listen to it."

The clock was ticking. I expected a knock on the door from the manager and police at any moment. As much as I wanted to stay, I needed to be on time to pick up my children. And then, still reeling from the kindly cuddling afterward – a transient cocoon – we got dressed, left the room, and returned to a parking lot still filled with shoppers carrying groceries to their cars. I couldn't help but marvel at my dramatic situation juxtaposed with their everyday chores.

We departed separately. I ate all the chocolates on the way home.

When I arrived at my neighbor's house, everything was fine. Save for the fact that I had put my blouse on backwards and was so informed by my friend. I laughed it off, breathing a sigh of relief. I didn't feel guilty, just enlightened. I had pulled it off. I felt desirable as a woman. I now knew that there were worthy men out there. I had thrown in my lot with an exception – Barry.

Realistically I knew that I had to stay with that Exception. I had to continue to make deals to go to Happy Hollow on the weekend. And I had to continue to care for my pets and to continue to ignore it when he teased the dog, taking out the leash and then just putting it back. As the boys got older, I had to continue to shelter them from what was actually going on in the home.

But when I was being sexually mishandled, I could now close my eyes and think of my one-time lover and one-time experimental fling.

Chapter 7

We were in bed, and Barry was ready for sex. I told him I was cramping, spotting, in pain, and needed to go to the doctor. He thought it was just an excuse and that my period had started. Menstruation had never stopped him before. I cried to no avail.

After intercourse, the pain was exacerbated. I stumbled to the bathroom, found some pads, and drove myself to the emergency room. My IUD had to be immediately removed. The ob-gyn on call discovered I had advanced endometriosis; infertility was a likely consequence. He affirmed that if I wanted more children, I should try right away after four weeks of abstinence following the removal of my IUD. He questioned future successful pregnancies.

After the procedure, I had to leave my car at the hospital and take a taxi home. I received no sympathy or apology from Barry. Barry had become an Albert Ellis disciple. He believed that you control your own destiny, and that you only got upset if you chose to get upset. When it came to sexuality, physical or emotional, I was used to facing traumas on my own. Although I tried to be stoic because I didn't want to be called "a whiny baby" in front of my boys, I became more agitated.

I kept thinking about what the doctor had said. Did I want another child so much that I could make another one of my movie deals? Could I handle the prolonged pornographic scenarios – the background hangings, the camera adjustments, his command to "smile!" – one more time? The inflatable doll, sperm dresses, pictures, and magazines remained in my life. All I had ever wanted was a white picket existence, but I had hooked up with a quasi- Marquis de Sade as a spouse.

My maternal drive was overpowering. I decided to try for one more baby, maybe a little girl. I knew this would be my last infant. I had to approach Barry about this the right way. So after his favorite dinner – breaded veal cutlets – and after the boys were asleep, I brought up the subject of another kid. My heart was pounding. I was sure he would be furious.

"You know I've been thinking about what the emergency room doctor said."

"Uh-huh."

"Are you listening?"

"The news is on."

"Let's have another baby."

"What did you say?" he retorted.

"Let's have another baby." I had his attention now.

"Are you joking? Aren't two enough?"

"No. It may be my last chance. And we're still in the baby routine."

He hesitated, considering what I had said. "What's in it for me?"

"What do you want?" As if I didn't know.

"Give me a few minutes." He went back to the news.

I left the bedroom and went to the kitchen. It was time for a cookie or two. Chocolate fix, please. Fig Newton.

From the other room, he called my name.

"I'll be right there." I swallowed the rest of my cookie and returned to the bedroom. The all-too-familiar black background curtain was hung. Already? At least I wouldn't have time to agonize over this new deal.

He must have been preparing this for a long time. Barry had hastily set up a porn film. Titled something like "A Mock Champagne Toast," it was the usual boring, non-plot tale. I had been up since 6 A.M. and found myself drifting off. But soon I was shoved awake.

"Delicious," he declared.

"What?" I stuttered. And then I realized that the actors were drinking cum. He couldn't be serious.

He was.

I had been asked but never cajoled to perform oral sex. Fellatio was an unknown entity. My naiveté concerning matters sexual was shared by many other women of my generation. President Clinton had not yet trivialized alternative favors.

It was another step in degradation. Quid pro quo. If I wanted another baby, I'd have to perform oral sex and drink the semen, while being filmed. Since sex was so businesslike and cold, I had few doubts that I could handle the new condition. The only problem was I had a very sensitive gag reflex, and even a test for strep throat with a tongue depressor or a dental x-ray made me retch. I knew Barry wouldn't care about my tendency to gag. I couldn't think of a way to negotiate out of his plan. When in doubt, do nothing. So I decided to press forward. How bad could it be? Mind over matter.

It wasn't long before I started to gag. I lifted my head and told him to let me please stop. He became furious and roughly held my head down. I started choking. I was having a hard time breathing. And then, still keeping his grip on the back of my neck, he ejaculated in my mouth. I had no choice save to swallow the bitter-tasting liquid. *I will not throw up*, I ordered myself. It would be many years before I realized that with love, kindness, and mutual consent, oral sex could be fulfilling.

Chapter 8

The night my daughter was born, Barry and I were arguing. He didn't want to drive me to the hospital. He thought I was bluffing because I didn't want to jerk him off. Then my water broke.

I resigned myself to calling a neighbor, dialing my friend apologetically – at one in the morning – to babysit my boys. Barry finally drove me to the hospital. He accompanied me to the labor room and left. Thank goodness in those days the daddy spent time in the waiting room until after the birth, in this case, of my beautiful baby girl.

I had my tubes tied later the next day to avoid future health risks linked to the great pressure that pregnancy had placed on my leg veins. Barry hadn't wanted to have a vasectomy, even though it was a quicker and safer procedure. He also advised me that one day he might want to have more children. Give me a break. I had Barry stay at home with the boys and not visit me in the hospital, requesting that he stick to their daily schedule, posted on the fridge, including pre-school snacks and items for Show and Tell. He told me that the waifs on the streets of Italy take care of themselves, which wasn't exactly reassuring.

My baby girl, Susan, kept me on my toes. Diapers, feedings, and nurturing. I savored each moment. Her brothers were so happy they even helped me care for her, holding the soap at bath time, folding laundry. I counted my blessings. A golden Labrador retriever, two parakeets, and a new kitten rounded out our group – "our" meaning the children and me.

A neighbor had asked me to give a home to the stray she found in a bush, thinking I would enjoy the company of a cat, my first feline. A week after the kitten arrived, Barry stood on the staircase in our house with a rope in the shape of a noose, pretending to strangle the struggling kitten.

"Stop it! Let him go!" I screamed.

"Just joking," he laughed.

I began to cry, unsure if he were teasing.

He told Michael, who had wandered into the hallway, "Your mother is an emotional baby." His favorite mantra.

At one year old, Susan had a serious bout with a fever and diarrhea, the first time she had ever really been sick. I was worried, tied up in knots. It took five days for the correct medication to kick in; for three days we had used an ineffective prescription. I was absolutely panicked. Barry scoffed at what he called my excessive concern. He let me know I wouldn't receive any time off from my wifely obligation.

Instead of begging and crying to leave me alone, I made myself lie still, not react, and get it over with.

Barry created a new nickname for me – "lazy log." Or L.L.

Chapter 9

Barry started calling me an "it" since I could no longer have children. He called me "V.V." for my unsightly varicose veins, a leftover from my third pregnancy, and "A.A." for my bra size.

While this constant ridicule made me feel inadequate as a woman, it also motivated me to stay in shape, just to prove him wrong. I made sure I remained attractive in spite of the constant temptation to snack with my three children, especially on peanut butter and crackers. Perhaps subconsciously I hadn't given up hope of escaping my marriage by attracting a new supportive husband and having a true loving family.

This was the era of Twiggy, the skinny supermodel of the time. I thinned down, fashioning my body after hers. My small boobs were in style. I wore mini-skirts and tights and paper dresses. I resolved that no one would ever call me "matronly."

I think Barry would have liked me to be matronly enough to be a good cook. I was when it came to basic kids' meals. I could have learned to go beyond macaroni and cheese. But I didn't. I wouldn't even make potato salad. Homemade potato salad with paprika on top. I didn't have a secret family recipe box.

For Barry's Christmas office party, a potluck, I offered to bring a dessert from the local bakery. I wasn't looking forward to the evening, but I had to go because of the boss' obligatory invite. Small talk and socializing were not my areas of expertise. I tried to keep a low profile and be ready to cover for Barry's gaffes. Several guests were getting tipsy from the free-flowing wine.

The buffet spread was filled with special dishes many of the wives had prepared.

An hour into the party, Barry clinked a spoon against his glass. He had a generous sampling of the various victuals on his plate. "To delicious potato salad!" he pontificated. "A toast to a gold-medal winning wife. *My* wife's expertise is opening packaged rolls and unwrapping store-bought pastries."

My cheeks flushed. Being humiliated in private was one thing. But in public? The other ladies nodded smugly and giggled. I poured myself another half glass of wine and stared at the Santa with reindeer centerpiece while everyone went back to their conversations. The Christmas gift exchange was about to begin.

Detecting how upset I was, the star potato salad wife's husband approached me, asking me if there was anything he could do to help. I declined his offer, but in an attempt to keep him talking so I wouldn't have to deal with Barry, I asked if he had any pets. Yes, he said, he owned two Newfoundlands: drooly, hunky chunks! He showed me a picture of his young son with the dogs.

He introduced me to his prize homemaker wife who was comfortably matronly – about thirty pounds overweight, wearing a loose-fitting grey pantsuit, looking older than her years. She seemed pleasant. Perhaps we could even have become once-a-while lunch buddies. But she had joined in the giggling at my lack of culinary skills. She said that she would be glad to share her potato salad recipe with me to make for my husband. I thanked her but told her that wasn't necessary; I didn't have much time to focus on food.

I was still seething at Barry's mockery when the idea came to me to prove a point. I had seen her husband look at me with a certain sparkle in his eyes and formulated a scheme to retaliate against Barry, even though, again, I would be the only one who knew what was going on. I did feel sorry for his wife, for using her husband as a pawn in my game. However, I was determined to prove that potato salad was not, in and of itself, the way to capture a man's heart.

When her husband asked if I would meet him the next morning for coffee, whispering to me as we refreshed our drinks, I replied, "Yes, if you bring your dogs." I adored giant breed dogs, and I was attracted to men who loved their canines.

The next morning after dropping off the kids at school, I parked at the café, ready for a dabble in flirtation, wearing a mini skirt I had saved for a special occasion. Skinny chic. I wanted to turn an ordinary morning into another mini drama. I was in control of my actions, without fear of being mocked by this man. I was becoming skilled at role-playing, even though I remained diffident. Deep down, I craved male validation.

Walking into the café, I saw him seated at the corner table. He stood and pulled out my chair; he had already ordered coffee. As I added Sweet n' Low to my coffee, my hand shook a little. I felt nervous, off-kilter. He seemed so amiable– as hungry for tenderness as I was – that any gentlemanly gesture, like offering me a taste of his brownie, overwhelmed me. The meeting morphed from a self-imposed, immature game into a pleasant interlude.

When we left the café to visit his dogs in the back of his pickup truck, it seemed natural to find a Motel 6, especially since he offered to bring the dogs in the room with us. There was an hour before I had to pick up the children. I stayed in the vehicle with the canines while he registered.

He was so calm and non-demanding that I found myself kissing him. This was unusual because for me, kissing was more poignant than any sexual act. My husband's wet, plunging, choking tongue had made me turn away from the practice. The emotional nightmare of my marriage had willed my body to go numb, my lips to close. But now I found pleasure in kissing.

Cooking wasn't everything. Who cared about potato salad? I was desirable in my own right.

Although we shared a few phone calls with neutral small talk, we had been together only that once. Family commitments complicate schedules, so we couldn't arrange another quick meeting. Besides, by this point, I didn't want to risk being caught. My children were older, and any non-routine action was risky. My thoughts centered on worries of car trouble or being seen.

But then my friend with dogs learned that he had to transfer to another firm out of state. I agreed to meet to say goodbye, an hour of farewell at a different motel, to assure our anonymity. To me, it was the courteous thing to do.

In the parking lot of the Motor Inn, he sat in his truck with his dogs slobbering over the front seats. With his scraggly beard, my friend looked like a comfortable teddy bear. His aura was of a nice guy.

I pulled into the space next to him. The dogs saw me and started wiggling and waggling. The whole meeting was, well, casual. I felt like I was meeting a colleague, no high drama. We made love in an amicable way. The potato salad study was over; I gained a boost in self-worth and was ready to return to Barry with a smug inner feeling. A harmless parting fling.

So imagine my surprise when, on the hotel floor playing roller ball with the dogs, I heard, "I want to be with you. I'm willing to leave my wife."

My heart started racing. I pretended to have not heard.

"Well?"

"Well, what?" I mumbled.

He repeated, "I'm willing to leave my wife. Would you and your children come with me?"

Shocked, I was certain I hadn't led him on to that extent.

"Sorry," I responded. "You have a wife and young son. A good life. Don't mess it up, especially not for me."

"We'll get a couple of Newfie pups. Are you sure?"

And so it ended. He left, with his dogs, son, and wife.

Over the course of the next weeks, whenever I walked with Barry to a movie or restaurant I kept hearing Judy Collins' song "Send in the Clowns." My life had become unfathomable. I enjoyed being mother during the day. At night, I was tormented by my husband. Even more distressing, I had taken to creating fantasies and acting them out with actual men. Who could be misled. I hadn't taken into consideration that my partners were taking me seriously. *The clowns are already here.*

I realized I needed immediate help with my marriage. I tried taking an assertiveness training class in order to stand up to Barry a little more. For a little peace. It turned out to be the only time I failed a final exam. My challenge was to enter a supermarket, buy a few groceries, and then tell the cashier at checkout I didn't want an item. Easy, right? Wrong. I was too fearful that the cashier would raise his voice at me for taking up extra time. Grade: F. That's how sensitive I was – except when role playing for an hour or two with an almost-stranger in a motel room.

Meanwhile my marriage was becoming harder to tolerate with its incessant kinkiness.

Assistance came in the form of an advertisement in the reception area of my doctor's office. A therapy group was being formed, led by two psychologists. The criteria for the participants: college grads, professionals, marital problems, and commitment to finding a solution, be it staying in or leaving the relationship. Fraternizing with group members outside of sessions absolutely forbidden. Six Wednesday evenings from seven to nine o'clock.

Well, at least I could get out of the house. It meant the children would almost be ready for bed when I left.

Barry was mildly amused. He had become very secure about his own actions in the bedroom, and so certain about my compliance and lack of sexual adventure that he didn't feel threatened letting me out to a supervised group session. He intimated that I would be found at fault for being upset by his sexual demands, which he thought should be taken as compliments.

That first evening I hesitantly walked into the group meeting room. There were eight chairs in a semi-circle, the male and female moderators sitting in front. In my hip paper skirt à la Twiggy, T-shirt (with "The more I know men, the more I love my dog" printed on it), and black tights, I was trying to see without my glasses. Vanity was my Achilles' heel.

I sat down next to a good-looking man with a beard. There were four women and four men as participants. Our similar qualifications for this group supposedly were fodder for bonding. A stepping stone for creating a congenial setting. This experience, harboring empathy as a goal, is ingrained in my mind. Even after all these decades.

After an introductory statement from all of us, it was confirmed that we were all conflicted about our marriages. We were all bright professionals trapped in seemingly untenable marriages. I, however, was the only female present who didn't have a well-paying job, and whose total personal spending money equaled twenty dollars a week. I had three children and a temporary credential to substitute for approximately thirty-two dollars per day. If the well-paid women (two were engineers) were afraid to leave their spouses, how did I fit in?

The second session was devoted to our own specific predicaments. I had drawn the Number Six spot. I listened to the stories: excessive drinking, philandering, hatred of in-laws, and money mismanagement – the orthodox causes of strife in a marriage. I lived, however, in constant fear of the consequences of saying no to Barry's odious demands, and my sole means of "earning" more spending money.

Then it was my turn.

I started with the sperm dresses. Then came the pictures and movies and hard-core pornography. I felt embarrassed and relieved at the same time that others knew of my predicament.

The circle was mesmerized. I charted my sexual routine from crying to stoicism to the baby deal, and shared that dressing up as a slut at times made me feel like one.

It was Number Seven's turn.

But everyone kept looking at me.

After group, the cute guy seated next to me was waiting at the door. He asked me if I wanted to get a drink. He was having problems with his third wife and thought I would be a great sounding board.

I reminded him that we weren't allowed to fraternize.

He laughed, "You must be kidding."

"What do you mean?"

"Nobody takes that rule seriously."

I passed on this invite. I had a bad feeling about his motive. Besides, in this type of classroom setting, I was programmed to follow the rules.

Throughout the remaining Wednesdays, the consensus of the group was that I should definitely leave my husband. Just go. With the three kids, and a retinue of critters. Logistics be damned! The lady engineer across from me with no kids and a chunky paycheck chose to remain in her loveless marriage. She had money, opportunity, and no dependents. She was despondent yet staying in the relationship. I, who had no money, no lucrative job, and a plethora of responsibilities, was being urged to leave. What was going on here?

Even though I was allowed to go out at night to this group, I had to return home immediately after the session or face a humiliating finger test to see if I were aroused.

Actually, humiliating is too mild an adjective for this violation. The first time Barry checked I was blind sighted. I froze. I felt like he was testing a piece of meat at the market. His fingers entered me harshly, prodding my sensitive flesh.

"Were you a good girl?"

"You're hurting me."

"Just checking."

If I felt wet, Barry demanded sex right then and there as my punishment for having naughty thoughts.

The last evening before class, the male psychologist in charge of the group tapped me on the shoulder. I had been listening, in disbelief, to a nearby conversation about an open marriage as a possible cure for feeling trapped. *Au courant* at the time. Although the late sixties and seventies were quite an era of sexual freedom, my strict upbringing and moral code prevented me from being comfortable in the sexual liberation movement.

"Yes?" I turned expectantly.

"May I see you for a moment after class in my office?" asked the counselor.

"Of course," I uttered.

I was more than a little anxious. Immediately I tried to figure out what I had done wrong. Had I offended someone? Had he seen me talking to Good-looking Beard in the hallway? I suffered through the last half hour of class.

I entered the counselor's office.

"Thank you for coming," he said.

"Is something wrong?"

"I think I might have a solution for your money troubles."

I certainly didn't anticipate this. "What do you mean?"

"You're kind and understanding. You could help men with sexual dysfunctions."

I couldn't believe my ears. He was suggesting that I become a sexual surrogate in a clinical capacity. I would be observed and aided by a medical team. Masters and Johnson had opened the door for this type of therapy. The pay would be excellent.

How strange to be asked such a thing. I was embarrassed and confused. At first I thought it must be some sort of joke or teasing. My ability to shut off my emotions, my expertise with black garters and fishnet stockings, my love for children and animals: this led to my desirability as a surrogate? Didn't he realize that my reason for joining the group was to clarify the sexual excess and humiliation in my marriage? And now I was being offered a job that required sexual encounters?

"Will these men have college degrees?" That's all I could think of to say. Sarcasm? Perhaps. Perhaps not.

"No, that's not a patient requirement."

"Sorry, I'll have to pass. I've got to go now." I was nervous about arriving home late.

"Good night then. Please reconsider the offer."

"Okay. Thank you for thinking of me. Good night."

I wasn't brave enough at the moment to tell him that from all angles – from the observation, to the sex, to the long commute to the East Bay – I couldn't handle it. I staggered out of the office.

Chapter 10

Time passed filled with the daily pleasures – and upsets – of stitches, chicken pox, and fallen Tinker Toy Towns. But as the youngsters got older, I began to fear they would walk in on Barry and me, or become aware of the sexual bullying. I didn't want my boys traumatized by their father's actions, or to think it was okay to mistreat women. I kept locking the doors, always afraid.

My occasional anorexia became worse because of the worry. Hunger pangs usually are not considered pleasant. *Au contraire*, being sated made me feel uncomfortable. I needed some control, somewhere; food was the easiest way to assert what little power I could. Hello, rice cakes and Tab.

Little by little I started receiving hints that others were noticing something weird about Barry besides his overt rudeness. Acquaintances started becoming uncomfortable around him. He was a like a dark cloud hovering in the room when he occasionally appeared.

Michael had a best friend in third grade whose mother was known to be over-protective. One day she told me that her son could only visit if I were the adult at home – not Barry. She stated that she felt uneasy around him; that was the best she could come up with.

"Please, understand, this has nothing to do with you and Michael. I am so sorry to have to bring this up."

"I do understand," I replied.

I knew Barry's lack of manners was too much for her. I had given up trying to cover for him long ago. When he did things like leave the room out of boredom, or announce that he was going to bed, people looked at me. I'd just shrug my shoulders.

Others were observing something off-kilter. When women were around, he would smirk in a flirtatious manner. At one neighborhood meeting pertaining to fences and landscaping, he oozed around the room and made non-funny remarks. He would walk up to a guy, put his arm around the guy's shoulders and ask if he were interested in wife-swapping. At the shocked reaction, Barry would quickly add, "just kidding." No one thought it anything but inappropriate, especially the wives. He didn't realize his behavior was more predator-suggestive than amusingly seductive.

Meanwhile, my parents moved to California when my father's job was eliminated. I had mixed emotions about their relocation. My parents' week-long visits, four times a year, were stressful. Mother's constant negativity about my life with Barry, whispered when the children could not hear, was debilitating. I had hoped that spending time with her in a different environment, without relatives to impress, would make her less critical of me. But that was not the case. She even harped on minor issues, like allowing the dog on the couch or my hairstyle.

Mother had an obsession with wanting me to cut my hair. I wore it shoulder-length with bangs. She would begin, "I think now that you have children, you should cut your hair."

"I like it this way."

"It's straggly and unattractive."

"Please, Mother, drop it. You know I won't change my mind."

She wouldn't stop nagging. Occasionally, when she would realize that she had pushed a little too far and I was really upset, packages of Fig Newtons returned to my pantry. I could resist the treats if they were not opened. Otherwise, a mini cookie orgy would ensue until they were all gone.

Mother and Dad were, however, doting grandparents. They fostered special celebrations for my children, taking them trick-or-treating, to theme parks, to ice cream parlors, and to the Santa Cruz Beach Boardwalk, money available thanks to a small severance package that my father received when he was laid off.

One time, Barry shocked the grandparents when he bought himself a candied apple from a vendor while walking ahead of the group at the seaside. He didn't stop to buy the children anything, just wandered along, taking bites. My father went back immediately to get the children theirs.

In like manner, at Sunday dinners, Barry would eat steak while the children ate hot dogs. As they got older and began asking for a taste of steak, I started running out of excuses to cover up his selfishness. He was the antithesis of the stereotypical Jewish father who adores his kids and gives them everything they want, even at his own expense.

Barry was not pleased with having my parents only a ten minute drive away. He remembered how they had whisked me out of our first apartment at the beginning of our marriage. Barry knew that I was becoming more and more unhappy in our union. My former quiet submissiveness to sexual coercions was waning. His power still intimidated me, but slowly I began verbalizing my reluctance: "Oh please, no, not again" … "Hurry up" … "I really hate this" … "I'm going to leave you." He took these utterings with a grain of salt. Sometimes he laughed; other times he pretended not to hear my pleas. But the message was out there.

I started thinking more seriously of divorce, especially since my parents were around to help. One night I threatened to call a lawyer in the morning. Again he laughed. Barry then told me that the children and I would only be able to afford an apartment in the tough side of town. The schools would be a hazard for my sheltered children. Moreover, he boasted that he had already emptied out our joint account and threatened to hire a hotshot lawyer.

It seemed likely that Barry wouldn't want custody of the kids, but the thought of him having them every other weekend, every other major holiday, and six to eight weeks in the summer, which was the normal agreement at the time, was unbearable to me.

My parents' proximity enabled me to return to teaching, relieving me of daycare costs. They cared for the children if they were sick and picked them up from school at the odd weekly dismissal times.

I was a daily substitute teacher hoping for a long-term assignment. It felt good to have other things to occupy my mind. My contact with colleagues afforded me a chance to envision a normal life on my own with the children. Or at least an opportunity to stand up to Barry. I started to think of myself as an individual, rather than Barry's puppet.

I could focus on students, lesson plans, and a small paycheck.

One catch in my road to liberation was that my parents weren't in the best of health. They were living a rather sedentary life, rarely even taking a walk around the block. Mother had high blood pressure; Dad had been told to reduce his stress and limit himself to one drink in the evening. My parents' medical concerns became material for Barry's sadistic barbs. Soon he returned to threatening to show my dad the pictures. I was afraid Dad would have a heart attack if I didn't please Barry.

I felt forced to cave in. It was almost a relief, not having to plot a rebellion right then and there. I retreated once more into the familiarity of coping with the marriage. And that would have been that. Until a life-changing episode on New Year's Eve 1974.

Shortly after we moved to California, Barry had joined a motorcycle club that met once a month for a Car and Driver discussion, followed by an afternoon ride through the mountains. Barry had developed a tight friendship with a fellow member, Brett, who was a chiropractor. He seemed pleasant and became an occasional visitor with his wife to our home. After they separated he started coming alone, as he did on New Year's Eve.

We played our usual board game, Monopoly. Barry took great joy in beating his friend with high end rents on Boardwalk and Park Place. I had gone bankrupt quite early and happily left the table to get a book.

I noted that Dr. Brett was drinking more wine than usual that evening. The children went to sleep right after nine o'clock; I had convinced them that since their parents were from the East Coast, that was our true time to revel for the New Year. I was nursing my white wine, having exceeded my usual half glass limit of any alcoholic beverage.

Between my small portions of food and low tolerance for booze, my dad had teasingly called me "the cheapest date in town."

While watching the T.V. coverage of Times Square countdown, I started dreading the obligatory midnight kiss with Barry. In the other room, the guys were laughing—and then whispering ensued. It no longer sounded like Monopoly chatter; their focus had shifted. I felt bad vibes.

So I decided to say goodnight before the New York ball dropped. With the children, I'd had an activity-filled day. We had seen a movie and stopped on the way home for ice cream. Michael was now eleven, Carl, nine, and Susan, five. I had wanted them to really enjoy the holiday. Barry had stayed home – resting.

I excused myself and started up the stairs. The children's rooms were across a small hallway from the master bedroom. As they aged, I worried more and more about their awareness of my marital woes. I automatically checked them and adjusted their covers. They were sleeping soundly. I lightly kissed their foreheads then tiptoed to my bedroom.

I locked the door, knowing that Barry could open it with a small screwdriver he kept handy. Still, it gave me a few minutes of security. I lay down on the bed, too tired to put on my nightclothes. I was on the verge of falling asleep, when I heard footsteps ascending the stairs. I wasn't surprised. I had known that my woozy state wouldn't earn me a sexual pass. I just hoped it would be fast.

I forced my eyes open to Brett locking the door and Barry adjusting his cameras, one for stills and one for movies.

"What's going on?" I mumbled.

"Show time," Barry said.

"What do you mean?"

"We have a great idea. It will take our pictures up a notch."

"What do you mean?" I was beginning to have a dreaded inkling.

"You told me that you thought Brett was attractive. Let's celebrate the new year with a threesome."

I tried to be rational even in my bleary, quasi-inebriated state. "The children are right across the hall."

"Don't be such a baby," Barry laughed. "They are all sleeping soundly. Come on!"

"No way," I responded half-heartedly.

"You have to – or else I'll show some pictures to you-know-who," he threatened.

Brett had remained silent. Now he walked over to the bed, took my hand and said, "Don't worry, I'll be gentle."

My head pounding, I felt trapped. Brett was more affectionate to me in that handheld moment than Barry had ever been. I just wanted the whole thing to be over.

"Do what you want. I don't care anymore," I said.

And they did.

Chapter 11

Two days later, I attended Michael's public school science fair with Carl and Susan in tow. Michael's project was photosynthesis, complete with a meticulously labelled poster. I walked around the exhibits with the other parents in a robot-like state. It was like my being was split in two. I chatted with the other moms about homework and field trips while at the same time, a voice in my head replayed Barry's bartering and sharing with his buddy.

Smiling on the outside and numb on the inside, I longed to erase the memory. Why didn't I fight more to refuse?

After the ménage à trois photo shoot, my heart affirmed that my marriage was over. I no longer felt any allegiance to Barry. He had given me away to amuse his friend. I was no longer a person but chattel. I was finished making excuses for the marriage, for staying. Finished.

I strove to be distant, really disconnect. My circumstances stayed the same. I still had to stay so the children could have a decent quality of life. My financial situation remained in dire straits. My parents had started to struggle with money – I noted the signs. When I asked my father to pick up some bananas at the grocery store for me, he asked for an exact count. When I asked for help buying patio furniture with canine décor, he mumbled about Barry's responsibility and having already committed this month's Medicare check.

I obliterated my emotional feelings when it came to Barry's demands. I earned my twenty dollars "allowance" as quickly as possible and tried not to react to his provocation. When I was taunted with having to live in a cramped apartment on the East Side if I tried to leave, I shrugged.

It was hard to shut out Barry during sex. I closed my eyes and imagined Robert Redford. I visualized rocking soothingly in a rowboat on a tranquil lake. I thought of my recess duty schedule. And I tried to block out his derision as he pounded away to his climax.

More often than not, I just counted – one potato, two potato – until he was done for the time being. The body turns off. The mind adjusts. But there is a price to pay. My desensitization nourished my anorexia. Hunger pangs during intercourse were the most effective coping mechanism. They proved I had control over something.

The next month I decided to enroll in a psychology night class to get myself out of the house. I got the children ready for bed, fed, and in their pajamas. It was February, the start of the new quarter at the community college. The only course that fit into my schedule was Business Psych 101. Not exactly my cup of tea, but, oh well. An escape is an escape.

On that first night of class I had a particularly tiring day and dreaded going home even more than usual. That night's marital argument at dinnertime had been about whether the kids needed a babysitter for the upcoming weekend. Friday night we were going to dine, just the two of us, at a seafood restaurant. Barry insisted we go, even if he had to drag me there! I thought Michael was too immature to supervise his siblings. When Barry realized how upset I was, he wouldn't back off. No paid sitter.

I was preoccupied with the sitter debate when we were seated for orientation at the community college. It was imperative that twenty enrollees signed up. Otherwise, the session would be cancelled. After three classes with the required number of students, any course was guaranteed. I did a quick head count to ensure that the class would last. Twenty-three! Three could drop out. Doable.

I reverted to my student mode and noted all the texts, supplies, and miscellaneous paraphernalia associated with getting an A, instead of a casual pass/fail. I didn't pay much attention to the other classmates. My head was still pounding with the onus of Friday's ultimatum. No paid sitter.

Class was dismissed a few minutes early. I gathered my belongings and headed to the parking lot. It was dark, and I started to hurry toward my car. A young man from the session quickened his step, approached me, and asked if he could accompany me to the car. I appreciated his offer. I didn't like being out alone in the dark.

He was quite kind; chivalry was not dead. I thanked him when we got there. "See you next week. Sorry, I forgot your name."

"Not to worry. It's Derek."

"And I'm –"

"I know."

I drove home with a smile.

When I arrived, I was prepared for the infamous finger test to see if I were aroused. Ever since the ménage à trois, I had felt completely removed from Barry. Barry, sensing my aloofness, had become even more possessive and wanted me on a shorter chain. In the future, I vowed to use a tampon to mask any telltale signs of arousal. However, that night I passed the exam with flying colors. Worry about passing the test had dried up any telltale sign of desire caused by the kindness of a cute stranger. Thoughtfulness was an aphrodisiac to me. Little did I realize that my life was about to shift.

Chapter 12

I t's strange; I'm finding it difficult to begin writing about this particular phase of my life.

It was wonderful at the start and devastating at the end. And there is an emotionally-charged P S., a storyline of which tacky soap operas are made. I toyed with the idea of searching for Derek online. But more than thirty years have passed. I decided to let the past stay buried. The odds of a meaningful reunion were nil. I couldn't even find a photo of Derek from that time. How bizarre. I wonder why.

At the next psych class, Derek had a seat saved for me. I wondered if good men outnumbered the bad. I appreciated the slightest courtesy because of years of disrespectful bondage. When Derek subsequently confessed to having followed me home to see where I lived, I was blown away. Such a secretive action would never have entered my mind. I couldn't have imagined that anyone would take time to check out anything about my life. I accepted Derek's invitation to lunch the next week; it would be another casual diversion from Barry. Just lunch. Why not?

We were to meet at an Italian restaurant at noon. I arrived first and chose a seat facing the front. It was a slow Tuesday with few customers. I jumped each time the bell on the front door chimed then tried to relax by thinking of a pack of dogs running on the beach, frolicking in the waves.

Derek walked in, so handsome in a clean-cut college way. Bowing to the trend, he had pulled his hair back in a tidy shoulder-length ponytail. He reminded me of a model in an Irish Spring ad (running over the moor to his love). I beamed. He had shown up.

I was up front about being married with children—and shocked to learn that he was eight years younger. I felt uncomfortable with this age factor. He had never been married, and I felt he would eventually want children. I remarked that someday he would be a great dad. To my surprise, he became philosophical. He remarked that the world was overpopulated; he had been contemplating a vasectomy for quite a while, way before he met me. A footnote to the times.

We talked and talked – for three hours. Over a half glass of red wine, I realized that I really, really liked this man. Romantic illusions exploded in my mind. My heretofore stoical heart started to pound. Derek did not proposition me immediately or take prurient interest in sharing sexual revelations. I felt I could trust him. I wanted someone to tell me it would be all right. I wanted absolution for my actions.

When he asked me if I were happy in my marriage, I answered, "Actually, no. Not at all." I told him that the New Year's Eve incident overshadowed my every day.

"Then why don't you do something about it?"

"Because there are blackmail pictures."

Two weeks later, Derek offered me a key to his house to use as a haven if I needed it. I was stunned and delighted.

Overwhelmed by the faith that he had shown in me, I found my sanctuary. I could use his home for escape during the day when the kids were at school and he was at work. Derek lived in the neighborhood of one district in which I subbed. It gave me great pleasure to sit at his table and have lunch or relax on his couch to read a book during a prep period. Sometimes he took an extended morning break and surprised me at his house. I was overjoyed to see him, and would jump up and fling my arms around him. It was the first time in my life that a man bear-hugged me; it made me giddy. I was insatiable for the sensation of sustained bodily contact.

"What are you reading?" he asked.

"Greek mythology for my afternoon classes."

"Well, don't let me distract you. I'll just sit here."

We sat, thighs barely touching. He never took advantage of the situation. And I felt better just knowing I could rely on a kindred soul. We had kissed goodnight only once, in the parking lot. On the cheek. I was being courted. It felt wonderful. I felt that someone had my back. Now I was ready to act. I could get out of my marriage, with Derek holding my hand. Derek had shown me there were decent men out there. I had found one. He could help me with my dad and any picture confrontation. I was sure.

First, I made an appointment with one of my former group's therapists. I needed a sounding board about the age difference. Even though Derek professed it didn't matter to him, in my heart I couldn't accept he would not want children. One could say I was asking for permission from an authority figure to pursue a relationship with a younger man. I thought she, knowing my circumstances, would advise me to stop seeing Derek. But to my surprise, she told me, without reservation, to continue the relationship, even if it were to last only a few months. If I understood her correctly: grasp the moment, and if the commitment dies, it still would be worth it for those moments of happiness. I, a born worrier, was given a green light. From a professional.

This time, with Derek as a cohort, I would ask for a divorce and go through with it. Derek vowed to help me find the infamous pictures and destroy them. At that point, we didn't realize that the photos were stored in a myriad of places, and that Barry had skillfully hidden the most damaging ones.

I was scared. I didn't even know how to begin the legal process. I had tried leaving Barry once before. With twenty dollars cash—this was before credit cards in my name—I had gotten about five blocks. Three children, one dog, a couple of birds, and one kitty. No money of my own. A husband who threatened me, laughed, and felt no regard for the children's welfare. He taunted me: Who would believe the words of an emotional baby who needed therapy?

To goad me even more, Barry loved to share "the infamous Valentine's Day's incident" with anyone who would listen, even though it had happened long ago, the first year we were married.

That Valentine's night, the phone had rung at 11:30. I knew instantly that something was wrong. It was too late for a casual call. With trepidation, I picked up the receiver.

"How could you?" accused Mother.

"What are you talking about?" I asked.

"How could you do this to your father?"

"Do what?" Already I was flooded with guilt.

"He's done so much for you, and this is the way you repay him?"

"Mom, what are you talking about?"

"How dare you forget to send your father a Valentine's card!"

I was speechless. With all my waxing newlywed problems, my mother was shrieking at me about a silly card. A commercial pseudo holiday card for my father no less. Unbelievable!

Barry motioned to just hang up. But I didn't slam down the phone. I listened and cried and apologized, as I was pre-programmed to do.

I was upset for weeks. Another few sessions with a shrink.

"Why are you so upset? Why do you care? Grow up!" Barry stormed.

How could I announce I definitely wanted a divorce? I decided to do so in a public place. Barry would be furious. Even though he shared me with his friend for sexual purposes, Barry still felt he owned me. I, however, had reached the end of my rope: my lifestyle with him was intolerable, especially since I had met Derek.

I called my parents and advised them of the impending divorce. They were relieved but not quite sure I would go through with it.

Barry and I went out for a steak dinner. That usually put him in a good mood. My oldest son was not babysitting; I was paying for a suitable babysitter with money from subbing.

After the tiramisu, my hands shaking in my lap, I cleared my throat. I could do this. I plunged right in.

"I'm really unhappy. I want a divorce."

He smirked. "Who is going to support you? We've been here before."

"Please, let's make this as easy as possible."

"In your dreams! I'll make your life a living hell. I have lots of money, and I'll hire the best lawyer. You can't even afford a paralegal. Good luck!"

We drove home in silence.

As we approached the driveway, he proclaimed, "I'm really turned on. I've bought you a new French maid costume. Can't wait."

I needed money for a lawyer. My only choice was to sell the diamond engagement ring that my in-laws had given me a year after Barry and I were married. It embarrassed them that I only wore a "cheap" gold band. I wound up selling the ring as quickly as I could, taking a loss at $1900.

I had found Derek, but I would have to resign myself to being apart from my children when they were with their father. I had never been separated from them, even for one night. Summer weeks without them were a horrendous thought.

My lawyer, unbeknownst to me, was a novice in divorce cases. At least he had forethought about protecting my daughter. Because of Barry's repetitive taunting about "devirginizing my daughter," he added a clause to the divorce settlement stating that my daughter could stay overnight with her father only if her brothers were there too until she was eight.

I look back with amazement at how uninformed and naïve I was during this crucial time when it came to legal negotiations. I could stay in our house, but Barry could deduct his mortgage payments from my alimony. He would get the tax exemption. Furthermore, after six hundred dollars, any money I earned subbing would be subtracted from his alimony fifty cents on the dollar. In a sense, I was being punished for working. Some mumbo-jumbo prevailed about his pension. I could not claim any percentage of it. I can't even remember why. At this point I just wanted out. I was so gullible, an easy mark, a woman in emotional turmoil.

I received minimum dollars in the settlement but maximum emotional support from Derek. Signed and dated. To be official in six months.

Barry resented moving into an apartment and leaving me in the house. When we met for a court-required paper signing, Barry made me an offer: an Alaska cruise to stop the divorce. When I refused, he shoved the stock certificates at me that he had he negotiated as part of the settlement. "You're ruining the family. Sign. It's all your fault. You'll be sorry."

The children and I planned a trip to San Diego after the negotiations. We were always a cohesive group, and there was little overt trauma when Barry moved out. Our southern California excursion was a coming of age milestone. I would be in charge. We were traveling by plane, and I was renting my first car. I would savor my independence. I would decipher any map. This challenge in my mid-thirties.

We enjoyed a great five days away. The small liberation made me feel proud. I had successfully led us to the beach at La Jolla, to an aquarium, to restaurants, and to amusement parks. I accomplished my goal.

There were some positive signs of a brighter future. Barry was in an apartment about ten minutes away. Derek and I were slowly getting to know each other. We were becoming a recognized twosome in our business class, with a lot of good-natured teasing about hand-holding and blushing.

At this point, Derek and I still were just "making out." He started spending time around my house. About a month after the official separation, Derek was looking for a tool in my garage, a wrench to help Carl fix his bike. In a corner, behind some cardboard slats, he discovered three boxes of pictures of me and Barry taken with a tripod. He decided to help me destroy them at his house, burning them on his barbeque grill. That way they would be completely eradicated. No chance of paste-and-patch. Ashes.

I accompanied Derek to his home. After all, it was my problem. I was scared. Barry would be furious when he found out. What would he do? He was still in the process of moving his possessions. However, it was too tempting an idea to reject. I never would have known what to do by myself.

While others grilled hamburgers and hot dogs, Derek and I grilled photos. The smoke rose, as did my hope. I did not realize—or I blocked out—that many other pictures and all the movies were not accounted for. We returned home: Derek rejoicing, I tentatively relieved.

Derek seemed to enjoy kid-oriented activities. We promised the children we would take them to play miniature golf. We went to Great America, rode roller coasters, and tossed dimes into fishbowls. Derek promised us that we would go to the Renaissance Faire in August. He enrolled them in soccer.

Meanwhile we savored our twenty-four hours alone, every other weekend.

I was head over heels in love. When Derek and I were intimate at his house for the first time, it was glorious. When we went to the kitchen for a snack of leftover cheese pizza, the aura became charged with electricity. When his fingers touched mine while reaching for a slice, I trembled. We knew our friendship was going to a new level, and we both felt trepidation, as well as desire. This could mess up everything.

Could I banish thoughts of Barry? Could he? Would the children call from their Dad's and ruin the moment?

I needn't have worried. It was splendid. Sex with a love friend was like being cocooned in a warm blanket. An orgasm while being kissed, exquisite.

Don't believe it when a woman tells you that she can have sex for sex's sake without a problem. We are programmed to love. It's much better than proving a point. All I wanted was to be cherished for myself, not for a lewd performance. My soon to be ex-husband had been turned on by control and manipulation. I didn't want any more "deals," or bartering, or neutrality. My future would be different. I had found my knight in shining armor.

Derek and I hung out at my house as much as possible. He suggested that we buy a waterbed, a fad of the times. One night, as Derek and I sat at the kitchen table while the kids were getting ready for bed, I nervously brought up something that was on my mind.

"Derek, we have to talk about my children."

"Okay. What's up?"

"I have to be up front. You can't stay overnight; I don't want the kids seeing you in the morning." I'd be embarrassed. They might become upset and pick up negative vibes from me, a mother raised in the Fifties. Wanting to be a proper role model, especially for Susan, I wasn't ready to take on society in general or my parents in particular.

Derek was quiet. He rose from his chair and seemed pensively serious. He approached me and grasped both my hands. He made eye contact. I panicked, thinking I had scared him off.

"Not a problem," he said softly. "I'd feel uncomfortable too."

I really loved this man.

We wound up at Mattress Town. A change of bed seemed a

necessity rather than a luxury. And the thought of undulating waves was erotically enticing. It was our first joint purchase. I was actually becoming optimistic.

Three days later this same waterbed became the center of high drama.

I had felt momentarily dizzy while choosing a bed but had attributed it to excitement. In fact, I was incubating the flu. A virus had been circulating among my sixth grade French students. I thought I had escaped the bug, but now I felt miserable and was running a fever of 102.5. My new waterbed was making me seasick to boot.

Unable to get out of bed without a bout of vertigo, I called Derek for a kind word. My parents had the children covered and were driving them to school. Derek immediately took the day off and came to help and walk the dog. I asked him if his boss were angry at the short notice. To which he replied, "You are, and will always be, my priority."

I mumbled a feverish thanks.

Derek placed a cold cloth on my forehead. It felt strange, yet exhilarating, to be coddled. What a contrast to Barry's routine of sex first, addressing medical concerns second—if at all.

My parents returned home after carpooling with homemade soup, bland white bread, and Ladyfingers. Imagine this tableau. We're upstairs in my bedroom. I'm ill and trying hard to stay awake. The prized waterbed is quivering, making me queasy. Derek and my parents are standing at the foot of the bed, the first time they are face-to-face.

Derek turns to them. "I'm going to marry your daughter."

Just like that, or was I delirious? I was astounded, yet relieved in a way.

My parents were completely taken off guard. I couldn't even look at them. Mother was disapprovingly mute. My father stared at him in disbelief. Dad was silent for what seemed like an eternity but was really only a few minutes. He was overjoyed that I was getting rid of Barry, but Derek was not exactly a suitable suitor. He was a computer hardware engineer – not particularly affluent, not exactly Ivy League.

Somewhat resignedly, Dad shook Derek's hand. "Make her happy," he said.

I think my folks had given up on their lofty expectations of a husband for me. At least I wouldn't have to broadcast the news.

"I promise," Derek vowed.

Chapter 13

My parents provided Derek and me a weekend off from the kids. We visited Carmel, walked the beach holding hands. I was happy; true love existed.

At night in the motel, we made love and experimented. Overcome with passion, I asked if we could try fellatio. I discovered that when I wasn't held down, the experience was quite pleasurable. No choking, no gagging, no sense of inadequacy. Free will cannot be overrated.

Two incidents further promoted our relationship – one in the eyes of my parents, and one for me – both of which encouraged me to believe in a golden future. Derek bought theatre tickets for a Tom Jones concert for my parents and us. It was a first. No one had entertained, wined or dined them before. Derek was on his best behavior. More importantly, he consciously avoided contradicting my mother. He read her expertly. We had become an accepted couple in their eyes.

The second event sealed my love. Derek went to the Humane Society and rescued a two-year old Border Collie. A canine is the surest way to my heart. Finally, I found someone who loved dogs too! My own dog adjusted to the newcomer easily and quickly. He had never cared about being Alpha dog. A true saint. In fact he let the newbie herd him around the house and yard. My children were happy with the new pup too. They became a five-member pack.

Surrounded by an aura of giddiness, Derek and I started looking at houses. Barry didn't like living in an apartment and insisted on selling our house. For tax purposes, I would have to reinvest sooner rather than later in another residence. Capital gains or some such jargon.

I had become a smitten teen in my mid-thirties. When the phone rang, I felt sixteen again, tickled that he had called. Amazingly, Derek felt the same. I was intoxicated without alcohol. Even mundane grocery shopping together felt like an erotic date.

Suddenly I felt the urge to become the homemaker that I had formerly ridiculed. I started a recipe box even though cooking wasn't on the top of my list, preparing his favorite dishes, from simple tacos to pheasant under glass. The key to Derek's house became my good luck charm. At times of stress, I wore it on a chain around my neck, a reminder of him on my flesh. My life seemed to have acquired a pocketful of feelings which the romantic poets glorified. I blushed often and giggled when he repeatedly declared his love. It was insatiable physical attraction, tempered only by the children's presence.

"Derek, I love you," I whispered to myself.

He wanted to spoil me, promising to buy me a Lamborghini someday. I didn't know what that meant. But it had a positive ring.

I hoped it was a rare Italian greyhound.

Then my bubble burst.

It was a Saturday in late-August. The children were with their father for the customary every other mini-weekend. Barry never took them in summer for a weeklong visit. My worry had been for nothing.

Derek and I bought take-out barbecue chicken and coleslaw. I set out the plates and noticed that he seemed distracted and rather nervous, not his usual loquacious self. He didn't engage in conversation or playfully touch my leg with his foot under the table. After the dishes were cleared, and a desultory dessert, I spoke up.

"What's wrong?" I asked.

"Nothing."

"You are awfully quiet," I persisted.

"Well, I just don't know how to tell you this."

My heart started pounding. "Just spit it out."

"I'm being transferred back East – to Connecticut. The company is setting up a new branch, and they want me to join the computer hardware division. I have no choice. We're talking at least three years."

Something akin to terror flooded my veins. This was certainly an unexpected, major glitch. What was I going to do? I didn't want to re-locate to another state: new schools, unknown neighborhoods, animal transport, credential qualifications, just to mention a few issues. I didn't even know if the custody agreement would allow it. And my parents wouldn't be around to help.

My dilemma was short-lived. There was a punch line.

"Uh, I think it would be best if your boys stayed with their dad. Your daughter may come with us."

I was flummoxed. Didn't he know who Barry was? I hadn't seen this coming. I was numb.

"Please, don't go," I implored. "I love you. Please stay."

"It's important for my career; it's the first step up the corporate ladder. I really have no choice. The Border Collie barked from the backyard. Derek continued, "I'm taking the dog back to the pound."

Finally, I found my voice. "I can never leave Carl and Michael. Please leave the dog with me. He can't go back to the pound."

I couldn't believe this was happening. Where had my true love gone? I tried once again: "Can't you find another job around here? It's too hard for me to leave."

I had just received my final divorce papers stating that I was now free. Derek and I were going to marry; we had been about to move into a new home together. I assumed a mortgage on the house and thus could circumvent credit checks, because there weren't stringent fiduciary requirements. The home was not situated in a single-mom-with-three-children-friendly neighborhood; the nearby schools were adjacent to several low- income apartment complexes. The children enrolled were predominantly street-wise. Four houses down sat a corner bar. Derek's home had been put on the market. There was a lot of repair work to be done on "our" new house. The backyard fences were not secure enough to allow the dogs out alone. The pipes were rusty. Without Derek, I felt abandoned. Vulnerable.

Derek had my answer. I would never leave my sons for anyone. At least I'd have his dog.

I didn't have the luxury of falling apart in front of my children. I had to perfect a placid façade, as if nothing were amiss. I had to pretend I really didn't care – it was just one of those things that happened.

Chapter 14

Derek was gone. And I was on my own, dealing with the children's welfare. Just when I thought things couldn't get any worse, Barry called, informing me that he had decided to look for a house within walking distance of mine. He aggravated me with the possibility of the kids stopping off to visit him after school. Especially my daughter, who was now over eight. Was this a bluff? Were we back to the days of Barry saying "just joking"?

Strangely enough, a few months later, my children wanted me to start dating, especially Michael. They noticed I wasn't having fun and suggested a night out once in a while on Fridays. They nagged. I protested. Derek's betrayal had numbed me.

On the Friday after Thanksgiving, a teacher colleague asked me to go out with her for Happy Hour at a local restaurant. I didn't know her very well, and I didn't particularly enjoy going out for Happy Hour, but I owed her a favor. She saved me an early morning run to the bakery and bought celebratory cupcakes for my class the week before the holiday. Anyway, I figured an hour's diversion, wouldn't kill me. Then we'd be even, and my children appeased at the same time.

We sat at a small table near the bar. I ordered a Diet Coke, my friend a virgin Piña Colada. Several men sat on stools nearby, and music was provided by a D.J. My friend was asked to dance by a suave thirty-something. I glanced at my watch – fifteen minutes to go.

In hindsight, everything in life is timing. The good, the bad, and the in-between.

Ten minutes to go, and an older man approached me. His name was André. He was slim, not particularly handsome, but not without a certain charm. He wasn't a Derek. He had a pleasing Canadian accent. I figured one dance would make the minutes go faster. He was a great dancer, especially to ABBA.

He asked if he could buy me another drink. I accepted another Diet Coke, I really don't know why. Most likely, years of conditioning to be agreeable accounted for my answers. I didn't want to hurt his feelings.

He definitely was a gentleman. We small-talked, innocuous chit-chat – after all it was Happy Hour. I told him I was a single mom and a substitute teacher with early-morning calls. I was often exhausted and fell asleep early at night. I omitted reference to Derek and his "only Susan can come with us" decision. When he heard I had children, André told me that he enjoyed being around children, observing them interacting or just watching TV. I thought, "Wow, he's really into children." I was subconsciously making a list. This was one positive to absorb.

One negative to absorb: his job.

André was a mechanic, a very skilled one. My parents would hardly be delighted with his blue collar status. The truth was that I, too, had a hard time accepting his lack of formal education, even were we just to date casually. We truly are the product of our early conditioning. However, he was quite socially presentable. But the main attraction was this: I was dispassionate. That was a good thing. On the heels of Derek's betrayal, I didn't want the highs because of the potential lows.

André and I started dating. We took a ballroom dancing class at the community center. I felt a little silly trying to rhumba, when I secretly wanted to be at home preparing for school the next day. We went to dinner several times. It was okay. We went to the beach, umbrella in tow, picnic basket filled. Okay.

Over the weeks, I discovered that he didn't have an overwhelming sex drive. Many times he just wanted to watch me masturbate. Fine with me. He was non-threatening in the bedroom: not pushy, not sex-crazed. No cameras in sight! This was the bedroom I was supposed to share with Derek; I could close my eyes and pretend I was with him.

Excuse the analogy: he reminded me of cardboard. Few demands, non-obtrusive, and vanilla in his desire. Derek had been my hot fudge sundae. Later, though, I'd find out that André was more like sandpaper than cardboard.

My mother antagonized André early in the dating relationship. She and Dad had taken all of us to a burger place on a Friday night. A couple who lived in their townhouse complex came over to our table to say hello. When Mother introduced André to her friends, she told them he was a mechanical engineer, instead of a mechanic. I didn't know what to say, so I said nothing. Even though he was trying to mask it, I could see that André was furious. He understood what she was doing; she was ashamed of his lack of college status. After all, he just managed an auto repair shop. I thought that was why he had bought the collection of *The World's Greatest Books*, from Louisa May Alcott to Émile Zola: to showcase his innate intelligence, and to prove, even to himself, that a formal education was not necessary. I never saw him read the greatest books, but they earned a prominent place in the living room. He also owned a collection of *The World's Greatest Classical Music*.

Meanwhile Barry kept harassing me. He made calls, laughing because he knew I was struggling financially. He asked if I wanted to "earn some money." His impending move would soon become a reality, and he intended to make good on his promise to be in close proximity to the children.

For my own living situation, it was the Seventies and living with André was not yet encouraged. So I waited for the proposal. I needed to change neighborhoods – that was a given. I could easily tolerate André.

And I received it, the proposal, I think. I actually don't remember the exact time or place. I know it was on Valentine's Day, because I was aware that this time I was rushing to marriage in three months, not three weeks. An improvement?

He had a pre-nup condition: we could get married only if all financial bills, including any mortgage on a future home, would be split 60/40. His reasoning was that since I had three children, there were four of us and only one of him. The fact that he made triple my salary somehow didn't enter into the equation. It would be more like a business arrangement than love connection, which was fine with me. My resolve vacillated between February and June. I had been advised not to accept the ultimatum which included no rights to André's pension. But Barry had moved only ten blocks away. I felt caught between the lesser of two evils. I chose money quirks over Barry's influence.

I had miscalculated André's money issues. They were more than quirks. My soon-to-be spouse had an obsession with mundane expenditures. He even boasted that he could eat for nineteen cents a meal (baked beans on toast). Nineteen times three equals fifty-seven cents a day. How does one react to such a boast? Congratulate him?

When we visited Monterey for a getaway weekend, he packed peanut butter sandwiches in his suitcase in case he wanted a snack, even though our accommodations were first class.

André even looked pained when he bought Thrifty ice cream cones for my kids, at fifteen cents: a real bargain. This attitude seemed so strange juxtaposed to his carefree luxury expenditures like skiing and traveling.

I rationalized that everyone had some sort of eccentricity. The money compromises seemed rather benign, compared to Barry's close proximity. Quirky with finances certainly bested hard-core pornography and blackmail. I liked André but did not love him. Never again would I risk a broken heart.

Sadly, I didn't realize the scope of the problem. Was it a case of low self-worth – I didn't deserve better – or the fact that I could never be approved for a loan in a neighborhood appropriate for my vulnerable kids?

I tried to see if I could do better in the business world, in lieu of substitute teaching. I passed my real estate license exam. But when I shared during an interview, at a lucrative broker's chain, that I was upset because my hamster was dying, I was dismissed summarily. During another interview at a newly formed real estate office, I was amazed that the interviewer queried me about whether I would spend any of my commission on my children's needs, like orthodontics. As if that were any of his business. I replied "of course," and he immediately lost interest in my application.

I attempted another venture: I matriculated in a shorthand/typing course, received an A, and upon completion was assigned to a law office. I lasted two hours before the lawyer told me it was too painful to watch me type. I couldn't remember the touch-method, I ruined the margins, I forgot how to change a ribbon. My six-week course at the community college did not help: the B I earned didn't transfer to an office. I hadn't had time to practice. My interviewer suggested I go to law school and then come back as an attorney. He gave me a fifty dollar bill telling me I didn't need to report it to the IRS, but to please just leave the office.

My last foray into a change of career was for a receptionist position at a printing shop. I was rejected because the employer felt that I was overqualified and too intellectual; in a nutshell, it made him feel nervous to have me around. He told me that it was a compliment, not to be upset, but proceeded to escort me to the door.

I weighed my options. I needed to move; I needed distance from Barry and from the current undesirables at the corner bar. There was no other way I could see to accomplish this – I had to remarry and stay in teaching.

The weeks dissolved. André and I found a house in a great neighborhood. Superior schools, separate quarters for the boys, and room for pets. My fiancé – once again I had passed on an engagement ring – was uninterested in the pets. "I could live with that" – a rationalization that became another one of my catchphrases.

While we were looking at real estate one weekend, André wanted to check out properties with a cottage in back.

"Why do we need that?" I asked.

"I have a great idea," he offered.

"Which is?"

"The children can live there, and we can stay in the main house."

This from the man who told me when I first met him that he liked to look at children's faces?

Then there was the "pool incident." I had always dreamed of a backyard pool. Especially now that the children were older. André said he would put in a lap pool on one condition: that I would swear not to swim in it while he was at work. I couldn't have any such fun when he was at his job, slaving away. I should have ended it then and there.

Years later, my friends asked me why I didn't just say yes, get the pool, and swim when I wanted to anyway. The truth? I was too frightened.

Weighing my options, I accepted a man's conditions again.

Chapter 15

I woke up the Saturday morning of my second wedding day queasy, a knot in my stomach. I thought of how things might have been different if I'd had more of a financial support system. My dad was making bad investments, hoping to make a monetary killing. The only killing he made was to his credit rating. I couldn't handle the mortgage on a new house alone. Two hours and we were due at the judge's chambers. I climbed out of bed with a heavy heart and glared at the clock radio. I could do this. I put on my short, frilly green wedding dress.

An hour later Carl told me he did not feel well. His stomach hurt, and he felt like he was going to throw up. My mother gave him some Tums and told him he would be fine. He wasn't a happy camper, but he proceeded to get dressed. In our nuptials finery, we drove to City

Hall. André was meeting us there with his unmarried sister who flew in from Montréal.

Making it through the vows, we were declared husband and wife. *Derek, it was supposed to be you,* I thought. I held back my tears as André kissed me, his bride.

The wedding party arrived at a local inn for a twenty-five guest reception. My dad, in a grand gesture that he couldn't afford, was footing the bill which included an open bar. As champagne flowed, Barbara Streisand's "Evergreen" started to play. I was tapped on the shoulder. It was Carl, looking ashen-gray. I knew I had to take him to the hospital immediately. The consensus of opinion was that the groom should stay with the guests.

I wildly double-parked in front of the hospital emergency entrance. My poor son was rushed into a cubicle and given fluids. There I sat in my wedding dress, worried and distressed. After the examination, the doctor motioned for me to follow him into the corridor.

"What's wrong with my son?"

"It might be appendicitis, but we need to make sure."

"Meaning?"

"Fifty percent of the time appendixes are removed for no reason. And then, umm well, look at the circumstances."

"What circumstances?"

"Your wedding day. Maybe he just wants attention."

"He wouldn't do that," I said. My head throbbed. I hadn't eaten all day, unless you count a couple sips of champagne. I couldn't believe that Carl was so ill. I kissed my son's hand. He felt so miserable and was sobbing.

What were the odds? What timing? Maybe it was an omen.

Around 4 p.m., all test results indicated surgery was necessary.

My parents, Michael and Susan, André, and a few friends were getting ready to leave the reception at the same time that Carl was wheeled into the operating room.

I sat in the waiting room – a mess to say the least. The E.R. surgeon arrived with an update just as my new spouse appeared, slightly inebriated, exiting the elevator. The operation had gone well. It had indeed been an almost-ruptured appendix. We were allowed to briefly visit, one at a time.

Carl was slowly recovering from the anesthesia. André asked him, "*Ça va*? How's it going?"

Debilitated emotionally and physically, Carl didn't answer.

"Your son doesn't like me," André somberly informed me. I was shocked. What was André saying? Did he expect my son to automatically welcome him as a stepdad? He was post-op, hurting and barely able to keep his eyes open. What had I done? My marriage was supposed to make things better for my children. And my new husband didn't have a clue about Carl's post-surgery reaction.

"Give me a break," I mumbled.

And thus began my second wedding night. Carl was asleep. Michael and Susan were with my parents. A neighbor was tending to the animals.

We, the newly declared Mr. and Mrs., checked into a local motel. It was 9:30 p.m., and I was as close to a migraine as I had ever been. Hungry and tired beyond belief, I was worried sick about my son. I just wanted to fall in bed and sleep.

All the *free* champagne had turned on my mild partner. It was our wedding night. So, in coping fashion, I decided to get sex over with quickly; I faked it.

I was on the verge of falling asleep when I heard him get up, shuffle, to the bathroom, and return with something in his hand that clinked when he put it down. My curiosity thus aroused, I opened my eyes.

There on the nightstand, on his side of the bed, was a glass filled with a floating object, like a laboratory specimen. I reached for my glasses to identify the item.

Dentures.

He had never mentioned this to me. I am not a shallow person, especially with my own imperfections. I was just taken unawares. I was so upset about the nondisclosure that I couldn't fall asleep. But after the whole hospital incident, I was afraid to further antagonize André on this wedding night. Would the good neighborhood be worth it? No use pursuing these thoughts. Marriage Number Two was a done deal.

Carl was released from the hospital within forty-eight hours, tired of being teased by the well-intentioned nurses about ruining his mom's wedding. He recuperated on the couch in the living room of the new house, co-owned by André and me.

This was to have been a marriage of convenience. My children were the salient focus of my future. I thought I could live with a low-key mate; it wouldn't be great, but it wouldn't be abusive either. I was naïve enough to think I would be able to co-exist without heartbreak or coercion. But a month after the marriage ceremony, I discovered more pitfalls.

The 60/40 arrangement, as I was to discover, was not clear cut. I had not factored in an important mathematical variable. To keep his forty percent down, he insisted that the lights be turned off immediately, the faucets turned off during teeth brushing, and his food not touched or eaten by my children. He doled out harsh criticism of my personal expenditures.

Michael was graduating from junior high and needed dress shoes for the ceremony. He had only one good pair of sneakers. As a teacher, I understood the peer pressure, when he told me all his friends would not be wearing sneakers. In bed that night, I mentioned my dilemma to André. He was furious that I would consider spending such an amount of money for a two-hour ceremony. "It's not practical!" He went on and on, so angry, and it wasn't even that I was asking him to chip in. However, his outrage made me back down. I still regret it to this day.

André passed another rule. If he did any chores around the house for me – for instance, change my car's oil – I had to stand there and watch. I was not allowed to read a book or play with my children or pets while he was actively helping me out. It wasn't pleasant for him, and therefore I had to put in my time to share in the discomfort. André felt it was all fair exchange; he wasn't interested in a power struggle, just an equitable trade.

Soon he revealed he was jealous. When I decided I wanted to take private guitar lessons at the house to be hip, à la Joan Baez, André agreed but insisted on sitting in on each lesson, worried about the teacher's attractiveness. He didn't want me alone with him.

I was having qualms, but André was content with the marriage. So very pleased that he bought himself a new sports car. It seemed as though his miserliness was not an issue when indulging in his own personal gifts. Pleased with the car, he asked me if I wanted a present of some sort. I opted for rescuing another abandoned kitten. Quid pro quo.

Meanwhile I reluctantly agreed to a one night trip to Lake Tahoe when André said we hadn't spent much time together alone. André had been bugging me for one-on-one time. I hoped that a weekend away would placate him; I could tolerate almost anything for one night. My parents would stay with the kids and critters.

Saturday dragged. We did not gamble, but we did seek out the cheapie buffets. I had no real appetite and was used to several small meals a day, just grazing. André kept telling me to eat my money's worth. He became more and more enraged when I was just picking at an oatmeal raisin muffin. He mumbled that he felt like shaking me, and I knew he was serious. I had married a deceivingly mild-mannered Scrooge – with a simmering temper, mistakenly choosing this man as safe.

I was relieved to awaken the next morning. We would be going home. I missed the kids and menagerie. If we left by eight, we'd arrive back by two in the afternoon at the latest. After a stop at the service station, we finally were on our way.

Let me state for the record, when I sit in the passenger seat, I am not very observant. Therefore, it took a while for me to realize that I didn't recognize the roadway.

"Are we taking an alternate route?" I asked.

"Sort of."

"What do you mean, sort of?"

Then he filled me in: We were extending our weekend and heading towards Yosemite. Knowing that travelling was not my favorite thing, he thought it would be good for me.

"Please turn around," I pleaded. My parents had not been informed of the new itinerary. They had made plans contingent upon our return.

"No way," he laughed. "Call your folks at the next rest area."

I was the victim of a broken promise, one planned way in advance. André had made a reservation at the popular Yosemite cabins. The phrase – "it will be good for you" – became a slogan I abhorred. André had unilaterally decided what I should do, and he exhibited total lack of respect for my parents. I felt so trapped. Yosemite it was.

Yes, we spent an extra night at a cabin. No, I hadn't jumped out of the car. Yes, my folks were irritated. They had to cancel their plans.

Yes, I endured.

I arrived home, livid and distraught. From then on, I always drove my own car.

Days passed in a sort of daze. Here I was, married again. It was not the 24/7 sexual abuse. It was not porn, photos, and humiliation. Yet I was once again in an unequal relationship.

Fortunately, my kids and I were close. When they were told not to touch his cheese, they didn't. They were polite to André but aloof. Looking forward to their new schools, they overlooked André's bizarre restrictions.

Mother stepped out of character and showed a lighter side. She started poking André's private stash of margarine while he was at work, doing a little finger dance on his American cheese slices.

Chapter 16

The first weekend in August, the kids and I had planned for a Saturday at the park. We enjoyed feeding the ducks. André frowned upon wasting stale bread; he wanted first dibs.

While we were in the throes of getting ready, packing snacks, water, and tennis balls, the phone rang. In a melancholic mood and exhausted from the preparations (not to mention consistent regret and masking my feelings), I almost didn't answer it.

To the sounds of children quibbling in the background, I picked it up.

"Hello?"

A familiar voice responded likewise. I couldn't trust my ears.

"Derek, is that you?"

"Yep, I'm back here in California. I had a hard time tracking you down. I went to your house and a new family had moved in. What's going on?"

"It's a long story. How did you find me?"

"I called your dad and asked for your number."

Thank you, Dad, I thought. He must have hesitated imparting the information since I was no longer single.

"I'm coming right over. Where are you?"

I was in shock. Had he changed his mind about my boys? Obviously, my dad had not informed him of my marriage; Derek didn't mention it. I wanted to see Derek so badly it hurt. I had blocked him out, but his voice precipitated a flood of emotion. He had been my only true adrenaline rush of love. Derek embodied high school and college romantic crushes, rolled into one. My ultimate soul mate.

Derek, so appealing, was a sexual magnet. He, who never experienced a sustained relationship—and I, who never felt the heady connection of the pleasure of the flesh—were meant to be together. Until Derek's shocker of a cross-country move, we were savoring the all-encompassing passion described in pop songs that before then had been only a myth. Even sitting next to him in a restaurant had turned me on to the point of wanting to be reckless in public. A single look would made me pulsate with desire.

"Where are you?" he reiterated. I realized he was waiting for a reply. Derek was back. I couldn't process it.

"Let's meet at the community college courtyard where we used to rendezvous before business class," I suggested.

"I was hoping for somewhere more private."

"We'll use it as a starting point. Just give me an hour to take the kids to my parents. We were going to picnic, so I have some arrangements to make."

"Okay, deal," Derek promised.

I was so nervous that I hardly knew what I was doing. I felt a mixture of sensual excitement, fear of André coming home early, and a quandary about what to do. Would this ill-advised meeting awaken dormant feelings? My current marriage had taken on the guise of a business deal gone awry. How could I explain my haste in remarrying? How could Derek understand that children had to come first, but that I truly had loved him? I became more and more unsettled.

I parked on campus, pulling crookedly into an empty space. The driver on my right would have to be skinny to get back in his car. Whatever. I had to get to Derek.

I saw Derek first, sitting on a bench with his back toward me. I would recognize his ponytail anywhere. Students hurried between classes, coeds lounged on the grass sunbathing. In the heat of the day, a water fountain in the corner was overrun by pedestrians and a queue had formed.

His familiar silhouette was almost too much to bear. The beat of my heart, my sweaty hands, and my memories of lovemaking fostered a suffocating feeling of vertigo. I thought I might faint. Well, that would be dramatic.

I inhaled and exhaled slowly. Twice. Then my feet moved as if by their own accord. I whispered, "Hi."

Derek turned and smiled. He stood up, and I rushed into his arms. He kissed me gently, and I wanted him so badly that it hurt. He felt so good. It was lucky that we stood in the busy college community.

How shall I continue without sounding saccharin sweet? I can't, so I'll just fast forward fifteen minutes. We joined hands and started walking.

"I realized that I made the worst mistake of my life," Derek was saying. "I want you all to come back with me. All of you – and that includes the pets! We belong together. I love you." He squeezed my hand. "Now, with the new job, I can easily take care of a large family. All of you."

I knew I had to tell him right then and there about my new status as Mrs., while meandering though the verdant campus on this beautiful day. It was now or never.

"Derek, there's something you should know," I said.

"What's that?" he murmured. "How much you love me?"

"Not exactly. Derek, I'm…I'm," I stuttered with emotion. "I'm remarried."

And the beautiful day disappeared.

"You're joking!" he said. His face became an abstract of confusion. "You'd never go back to Barry!" He began to realize I was serious.

"It's someone else." I was crying now. "I don't love him. I only love you."

Derek blanched. He was still perplexed. The anger had not yet set in.

"Why did you do it? It's only been several months. I flew back to California for you."

"I'm so, so sorry."

And, so it continued for two hours, me apologizing, and him trying to reconcile the unfathomable truth.

"Leave him," he offered. "All of you can come with me. Please."

Here I go again, I thought. I feared relocating my family with school about to start. Who knew what the teaching jobs would be like back East? He had left me once; he could do it again. Should I extricate myself from 60/40? Barry surely would laugh if I got another divorce. It was a momentous decision: What should I do?

And the only words that escaped my lips: "Do you want to see your dog before you go back?"

"No," he answered curtly. "But we should make love for old time's sake at least."

I started to cry. He sounded angry, sad, forlorn.

"Not a good idea."

I knew if I were to do so, I couldn't stand not being with him. I wanted no more drama.

My only solace was that he didn't want to see his dog. How could he not? I tried to focus on this lack of caring for the Border Collie. I exaggerated this flaw. In truth, my heart was breaking again. I needed something negative to focus on.

He didn't look back when I walked away.

I returned home befuddled. My parents took one look at me and remained silent. Everything in life is timing. Derek had been two months too late.

Chapter 17

I look back at my second marriage as a two and a half year bad date. Beware ladies all. A 60/40 arrangement like mine never works out. You become resentful. Very resentful.

I began to resent his interference with my children; he didn't enhance their lives. They started "touching" André's sacred cheese in the refrigerator. They never ate any; they were too scared of his disciplinary restrictions: early bedtime or painting the grey concrete in the backyard green. We thought of him not as a stepfather but a boarder in our home.

When my birthday arrived, André's present to me was a slightly ripped beach towel that he found at a boutique in town. It had been reduced to fifteen dollars, but the pattern included a dog. The children and I didn't know how to react. They were embarrassed for me, and I wanted to disappear.

Mr. Forty Percent had become the head of house just by dint of being male, not by any largesse or caring. He started checking my purchases for what he considered extravagance. Fancy Feast cans became contraband under my blouse.

I resisted becoming a twice divorcee, accused of frivolity, flakiness, and questionable judgment. Barry would have a field day, saying, "I told you so." My white picket dreams turned charcoal.

I braved it out for a while, but the irony was about to do me in. Here I was struggling financially more than I had struggled while single. I was constantly under surveillance. There were other discomfiting, seemingly trivial, incidents. One of my cats disliked 60/40 intensely. Whenever this feline saw André, he defecated in front of him. The cat was relegated to one room, with a sign on the door reading "Do not let out." The dogs were allowed in the kitchen only. T.V. programming was limited to PBS Channel 9. PBS complemented *The World's Greatest Music and Books* as proof of his intellect. I had to fight for the right of early Saturday morning cartoons for my children. Even "Tom and Jerry" became a point of contention.

In November, at Thanksgiving dinner hosted by André, my parents were shocked at the tiny eight-pound turkey served for the seven of us. My father turned red with anger because stingy 60/40 had figured out the cost, down to the last portion – one pound per person. God forbid someone wanted seconds! And my father had offered to provide the turkey the week before. André had vehemently declined, wanting to play the host.

What kind of role model was I being now for my daughter? A weak hausfrau. I was sick and tired of being told what to do: peering under the hood of my car while he checked the engine, or having the gall to weigh in on extracurricular activities involving fees for the children. He wasn't even the one paying. Or contributing. Would I ever be able to read a novel again at my leisure?

I accepted a low-paying job teaching in the private sector. Substituting had become too stressful with its last-minute calls in the early morning. As map reading was not a strong point of mine, the various locations also proved stressful. Meanwhile, my own kids qualified for reduced-rate lunch. Michael was too embarrassed to accept this. It took me a few weeks to find out that he was skipping lunch altogether.

Barry was paying the minimum support and not indulging them. He certainly did not spoil them with trips, luxuries, or extra cash. He felt that such actions would benefit me. He didn't want child support to help me, their mother, in any way, to contribute to rent, food, or clothing. Although Barry was entitled to custody for the entire summer, he only took the kids for four consecutive days when his mother was in town. Once. Thereafter, he stuck to his brief weekend visits. Barry told me if I needed additional money I should ask André.

60/40 didn't help.

Marriage Number One began with tears and ended in flames.

Marriage Number Two began with a shrug and ended with a shrug.

When the time came to separate, I needed to buy André out. In order to keep the house, I had to come up with a lump sum that represented the potential capital gains if we sold the house. An appraiser determined that I owed him $25,000, accounting for the appreciation of the property. My parents came up with $5000. I felt guilty about taking it from them, even though they had come to dislike André's miserliness as much as I. I had no choice but to take out a second mortgage on the house. I would be struggling again. However, at least, I would struggle alone. More importantly, I would be able to read any book, my beckoning beacon, without posing for pictures or watching someone fix a pipe under the sink. I could supplement my income by tutoring on the weekends.

I needed to break the news, and I knew he'd be furious. After dinner, on a Friday evening, I asked André to come into the den to talk privately. He was washing his own dishes, so complicated had become the 60/40 arrangement.

"I can't handle our marriage anymore. I want a divorce." I didn't like his body language, the opening and closing of his fist.

"You have a contract. We signed it."

"I know, but I thought it referred to house expenses, like the phone bill and mortgage. I didn't know it would include food and separate… everything. It was a mistake. It's over. I'm sorry."

"I have a strong urge to throttle you," he said. I was a little frightened but knew my next words would soften his wrath.

"I have the entire sum to buy you out." That's a lot of baked beans, I wanted to add, but knew not to push him further. He was assuaged by the thought of a bulk payment for his investment in the house.

I counted the days to André's departure. When we appeared in court for the interlocutory decree, my lawyer found it amusing that André's female attorney had creases on the back of her skirt. He made a sexist joke – the gist was how sloppy and unkempt she appeared. Her hair was stringy, and she wasn't too attractive. I found no humor in his comments and wanted to tell him he was being rude. It turned out that the joke was on him. My well-pressed attorney had forgotten some critical papers at his office that needed to be signed.

And as a result, André was permitted to live in my house another three months before the new court date. He didn't want to pay three months of rent anywhere if he didn't have to. He stayed put. It was beyond awkward. I had to perfect a new kind of compartmentalization. Imagine having to coexist in an environment with someone you can no longer stand, and who is furious with you for disrupting his life. Or forty percent of it.

How did I become a woman who had to divorce two husbands? I was great with children and animals. Obviously not so with men.

Peace will be enough, I thought.

Chapter 18

Two years after being divorced for the second time, I was still teaching in the private sector. My children were busy with school and activities. Money was a constant concern, but all food was for the taking, and we could even watch mainstream TV.

I never contacted Derek again or tried to find out if he were married or not. The pain of his betrayal haunted me. If he left me once, he could do it again. I couldn't risk exposing my children to another breakup. I wanted to keep Derek a dream lover and remember only the love we had before his transfer. It was time to look forward not backward.

Divorce Number Two was a green light for Barry to renew tormenting comments over the phone. He knew that I was hurting for money and began offering big bucks for new photos. I tried to ignore him. One particularly cold month, my utility bill was high. The children and I were tired of wearing double sweatshirts in the house. My credit card debt was rising. The next time Barry called I was trying to figure out if I could do more tutoring on Sundays, not the most popular day for studying. I didn't hang up fast enough; I heard him say, "I have a great deal for you. You can't afford to pass on this one."

I was skeptical, but I listened. Barry outlined the conditions: forty-five minutes only, if I would reprise my "modeling" in a former outfit, a saved soiled black cocktail dress. One photo only. No movies. He'd take care of my PG&E electricity bill for the month. Just forty-five minutes.

I rationalized my acquiescence: Theoretically, I reasoned, there was no immorality involved. After all, he was the father of my children.

We met at his friend's apartment, borrowed for what I called the "PG&E assignation." One look at Barry, and I sensed a drastic change in my perception. I could barely tolerate the feel of the fabric when I slipped on the familiar dress. A few years away from him had changed me. Again, I thought it would be easy. Again, I'd just tune out. Again, I was mistaken. The reprieve had modified me. *Let it be over, let it be over,* I chanted to myself. I couldn't even plead out loud. It was the longest forty-five minutes ever. I took my cash payment, full of shame, feeling unclean, even though these actions were for essentials.

Never again.

Never again, Barry.

I call the following years my second, supposedly mature, foray into the dating scene. I was encouraged to socialize by my immediate family, especially my mother and sons. Michael and Carl thought I should be enjoying myself instead of grading papers all the time.

Sound familiar? Mother kept telling me that dating was the normal thing to do. Or, perhaps I wanted to show Barry that I was still desirable to others.

Sample A. A former sheriff from Montana. Burly and rugged, an outdoorsman, and a heavy drinker. His companion was an extraordinary German shepherd: intelligent, and loyal. I adored him – the dog that is. We met at a singles' bar. When we danced to "A Horse with no Name," he instantly got an erection. He told me that the last time that had happened was at a dance in junior high. A month later, he was picking me up at school in his Jeep. I felt like I was living in a western drama. In a word, he was macho. Sample A liked my kids and was polite to them. Before we went away for our first weekend, he told my daughter how much he loved me to assuage any of her qualms.

We went to a motel overlooking the ocean, near the boardwalk, to celebrate our five-month anniversary. I was so happy. When we entered the room, he placed his suitcase on the bed. It seemed heavy. As he opened it, instead of clothes neatly folded, I saw a variety of bottles of booze. Gin, vodka, beer…

"Oh my god," I said. "Where are your beach clothes? I only see bottles! Have you lost control?"

"Nope, I'm totally in control," he tried to reassure me. "Come here, woman." He opened his arms for a hug.

"I don't believe you. It looks suspicious."

"That's your problem, not mine. In fact I've experimented. Last year for three months, I only drank beer. I repeat, only beer. See, I'm in control. Only beer."

That same weekend he placed a promise ring under my pillow. It had been in his family, and it was a token of his sincerity. He liked kids and dogs. He liked camping—really, he liked drinking in the woods.

His mother, who lived close to my home, continually warned me that her son was not suited for me in character; she worried about my future happiness. He had been married three times. But, look at me – I was a close second with two divorces of my own.

We had planned to go to Reno in a few weeks, and fortunately, yes, fortunately, I caught the flu – a by-product of teaching. I had an inkling that he wanted the getaway to turn into an elopement. However, with the postponement due to illness, we had to wait a while to coordinate school holidays and my parents' schedule. Mundane matters trumped romantic weekend escapes.

On the next Wednesday, he was supposed to come over for the evening and take us to Chuck E. Cheese. But around four o'clock he called to cancel because he was not feeling well. I offered to come over and take care of him, but he said that he was just going to sleep. He'd see me the next day.

My daughter had an idea. "Why don't we bake him some cookies and surprise him?" Her enthusiasm affected me. So, peanut butter with chocolate chip cookies, warm from the oven, were to be delivered. We were both excited. Susan loved surprises.

An hour later we drove to his house, both a tiny bit nauseated for we had "sampled" quite a bit of the raw dough. It was his mother's bingo night so I knew he would be alone. We softly knocked on the door, and his dog barked a greeting. (A note tied around this pup's collar that said "I love you" and delivered with slurpy kisses had jump-started this whole romance.)

When he opened the door dressed in his good shirt and jeans, he didn't look sick. Standing behind him was an attractive blond in a halter and short shorts, holding what appeared to be his special martini. I immediately registered that she had big boobs and no varicose veins.

I realized that my daughter was watching my reaction – which would have been much different if I had been alone.

"We brought you some home-baked cookies." I thrust them in his hands. "I didn't realize you had company." My face turned red with embarrassment.

"Hey, thanks. This is an old friend who just happened to be passing by on a business trip."

Yeah, right, I thought.

"Both of you come in, and we'll have a cookie party. I'm feeling much better."

"Sorry, it's a school night. Enjoy. We're out of here."

I didn't cry until two hours later, when the kids were asleep.

A betrayal is a betrayal. I returned his promise ring.

His mother was right.

Sample B. We met at a singles' dance for college grads. He was good-looking and had graduated from Middlebury, a flashback to Ivy days. We danced. When he asked me to come home with him to see his dog, I thought it was a variation of the hackneyed standard seduction line: "Come see my etchings." But he assured me that he had a beautiful Rhodesian Ridgeback.

Since we lived in the same neighborhood, I thought I'd take the chance on his sincere intentions. I loved Rhodesian Ridgebacks. I followed him home. The first thing I heard while I was pulling into his driveway was barking. The welcoming type. I loved her on sight – Samantha was her name.

Samantha forgot her boundaries and jumped on the bed to join us. I laughed and labeled the incident droll. Not so with Sample B. He scolded her and put her outside. That upset me to no end. I kept saying it was my fault, because she thought I was inviting her to join us. Sam's incessant whining at the sliding glass door interfered with our lovemaking. I left as soon as I could. He was truly annoyed that I wouldn't stay the night, even though I had warned him ahead of time that I would leave at eleven o'clock. He came up with a lot of reasons why I should prolong the evening, the common male challenge to try to keep me longer than I wanted to stay—perhaps in order to prove I cared for him.

In a moment of weakness and desperation to leave, I promised to make him his favorite snack for a Sunday picnic the next day: deviled eggs. I would ask my mother to make them, in addition to her usual casserole offering. I preferred writing poetry to cooking. And I still had my Twiggy persona. Deviled eggs were not appealing to me. Who would indulge in mayonnaise?

When I delivered the gourmet snack, his house smelled of bacon. As a newly converted vegetarian, I believed in "live and let live," but I could not tolerate anyone eating bacon. Especially the odor. I have known some very smart pigs of the four-legged kind.

Throughout history men have abdicated thrones for love. I lost love because he wouldn't give up bacon.

I'll juxtapose *Samples C* and *D* because they both involved food.

C was a Ph.D. in Archaeology but didn't feel comfortable around animals. Tired of the meat market bar scene, I met him at a synagogue wine-tasting event. He posed as a wine connoisseur and went on and on about different vintages and informed me that the highlight of his day was his first sip of wine in the evening.

In my heart, I knew that the relationship was doomed from the start. The first time he visited my house he put on disposable Playtex gloves! It looked like he was readying for an ob-gyn pelvic exam. Was it a joke? Foreplay? No, the kids were home. It turns out he was a germophobic, from dust, to cat hair, to dog drool.

That was the beginning of the end. The end of the end occurred because of my guinea pigs. C was with me at the supermarket. I was buying Romaine lettuce for them. A considerate clerk told me there were scraps of veggies in the back dumpster. I could help myself to the leafy leftovers and save some money.

When C accompanied me to the back of the store, his eyes lit up. This affluent man started raiding dumpsters – cantaloupes, carrots and other edibles mixed in with the greens for his own consumption. The free throwaways turned him on. And he was proud of it. The kids and I didn't want to eat at his apartment anymore – especially salads! "Where had that lettuce or broccoli come from?" we worried. I had visions of another 60/40 variation.

Sample D merits only a few lines. He was more of a father figure to me, sort of average-looking. His lure was that he had raised a wolf cub and a Samoyed pup together to compare and contrast their socialization. He spoke of marriage after a month. With one stipulation: I had to sit with him for three meals a day, for a minimum of one hour each. He had misgivings about my grazing, quick repasts. He couldn't reconcile my habits with his own schedule that divided the day by the traditional breakfast, lunch and dinner.

Conditions begone! No more musts. No more deals. No more men telling me what I had to do.

Chapter 19

Since I was without a steady partner, Barry wanted to get together with me, either in public venues or when he was alone in his house. He had inherited a lot of money, and he tried to lure me with a life of leisure. I didn't know whether to laugh or cry about this.

We were seated at an outdoor patio of a deli, meeting to talk about colleges, when he pleaded his case. "I really want to put our family back together," he began with a mouth full of roast beef.

"You've got to be kidding," I replied.

"No, really. I will build you a spa." Sarcasm was noticeably missing; he meant what he was saying. When he said, "I'll even help your parents out financially if necessary," I understood that he truly wanted me back.

I stared at Barry. He was serious. Sure, I was struggling, but did he really think I would return to his control? I was tempted to ask about his sexual conditions but thought it unwise. I didn't want to send mixed messages. I just sat there for a few minutes. Then I excused myself and instead of heading towards the ladies' room, I exited to the parking lot.

Before I continue my narrative, I have to inform the reader that I had decided not to tell my children of their father's abuse. All the self-help books I read, and all my friends, advised against any extreme form of negativity shared with the kids regarding an ex-spouse. Even my parents didn't know the extent of my mistreatment. Was this the right course of action: not speaking out? Staying mute while their father reiterated that I broke up the family as if I had been acting on a whim? I will never really know.

Laws were slowly changing around this time; women were "allowed" to say no to sex with their husbands. Non-consensual acts? Rape. Unfortunately, the ruling had been too late for me. But this "no" clause made me feel justified in divorcing Barry. I felt validated; it wasn't my fault. I had the right to be in charge of my body, married or not. Yet I wouldn't have had the nerve or resources to take Barry to court. And the children probably would have been devastated, especially my daughter.

Meanwhile the secondary school years evoked drama. My sons were quite good-looking. This was the start of the era of girls pursuing boys, even calling boys – unheard of in my time.

One Friday night, the bell rang. I heard giggling outside. Michael and Carl rushed to the door, saw me, and stopped short.

"Hey Mom, please hide in the bedroom," they chorused.

"What?"

"You'll scare the girls away. You're a mother and a teacher – you'll correct their grammar!"

"In your dreams," I laughed. "I refuse to hide. Next you two will have me crouching behind the sofa with the dog."

My poignant birds and bees presentation for teens was classic. The three kids were at the table, embarrassed in anticipation of any facts of life discussion. I opened with a declaration: "I only take in stray dogs and kitties. No babies. Be careful. Any questions before I continue?"

"No, Mom. We're out of here." Chairs scraped. I was alone at the table.

Chapter 20

It seemed like everyone had moved forward but me. Barry found a steady lady friend. They met at a singles' dance sponsored by Parents Without Partners. She didn't have any children but figured it would be a safer environment than a bar, aka a meat market.

I met her at a family celebration, Michael's birthday. My children asked their father to attend, hoping that we could all get along. Watching Barry and his plus-one interact, it was an enigma to me why she dated him; he was caustic towards her, joking about her old-fashioned hairstyle, for instance. Maybe she thought it was a sign of affection. She was nice enough, attractive enough, and truly polite. She was from southern California and had always worked in a flower shop. The only thing I had against her was that she gave Barry credibility. I felt that the truth about my history of abuse lost its plausibility because of her commitment to him: if she were so acceptable then my accusatory claims would somehow seem untrue. I sat at her table at this contrived gathering. Ladyfriend was okay at small-talk; I have to admit I sort of liked her. She certainly was not a floozy. That would've been easier. Barry now had proof of eligibility. Ladyfriend wouldn't be here if Barry weren't a decent guy.

To this day, I have yet to ask her about anything kinky in their relationship. I hesitate – she's too proper. Besides, she met him after his prime. He was starting to have medical concerns. Maybe Internet porn was enough for him now.

Ladyfriend was lucky that I didn't want him, I guess. Barry still provoked me with phone calls, either asking me back or threatening to put his remaining pictures on the computer. I was just starting to heal from his domination. Still, with Ladyfriend's imminent plan to move in with him, would anyone even trust me if I told the truth about Barry? The moment for disclosure had long passed. Would anyone really care?

When my boys turned eighteen, they were given the ultimatum by Dad to live with him or forgo any help with college tuition. He wanted a show of loyalty, at least that's how I interpreted it. Barry wished them out of my house. Michael and Carl were conflicted about accepting Barry's terms. They were perturbed. I reassured them that I understood. I didn't want money to become a burden for them. There is nothing worse than counting pennies or accruing debts. So I pretended that I was fine with the stipulation. I wasn't. It hurt.

Susan didn't move out. She called his bluff. She stayed with me, and he paid her tuition anyway.

Barry had a soft spot for Susan, the grown-up. After graduating, Susan planned to marry. Barry pledged to finance the entire bridal reception for her. Carl trained nearby, testing the waters as a paramedic. Michael was returning to California after earning a Master's degree in Science from Tufts, just in time for his sister's wedding.

Her magical day arrived. Susan decided on a low-key venue: a local restaurant with a specially flowered chapel area. After the vows, kiss-the-bride, and appetizers, it was time for the traditional father-daughter dance. The D.J. started playing one of the signature songs from *Fiddler on the Roof,* "Sunrise, Sunset." *Is this the little girl I carried?* I became silently incensed at the lyrical implication of father-daughter bonding. This was the little girl he didn't carry. He didn't watch her at play. It was only after she became an adult that he actively resurfaced in her life.

I had invited a close female friend as my plus one instead of a date because I could never trust what Barry would do or say when we were thrown together at any event. My friend, aware of the true particulars of my first marriage, joined in my discomfort being in proximity to Barry. Our unease intensified when his chiropractor friend – Dr. Brett from the ménage-à-trois photo session – asked me to dance. I didn't know what to do. I finally adopted a façade of equanimity and endured the fast-paced, non-touching "Flashdance." The music was so loud we didn't talk. Even so, it wasn't pleasant. He then asked my friend to dance; her refusal was so chilly that he did not approach us for the rest of the night.

All the other wedding guests were having a great time. I loved my new son-in-law and was happy for my daughter. It is a foregone certainty that a daughter needs to love her father. And Barry really did care; that was obvious. Once she was over eighteen, he hosted dinners with her. He and Susan shared a love of cooking. But her special moment was diminished by my personal black cloud.

After Susan's wedding, there was another consequential occasion. The family was gathered at Michael's housewarming. It was his first home, and he was very proud. He especially loved the backyard, already installed with swing set, sandbox, and slides. Michael glowed as he conducted tours of his home.

In addition to Michael's M.S. in computer science, he brought back a wife from the East Coast and a baby son. I was a "G." Could I really be a grandma? I imagined a gray-haired granny rocking on the front porch, knitting, with a cup of herbal tea by her side. I got over it, however, when I met the baby. Although I still like to refer to "my little G's" – "Grandma" just rolls off my tongue. Well, somewhat.

While I was single-dipping in the guacamole, Michael asked if he could see me on the patio to talk. He sounded rather serious.

"What's up?" I asked.

I was finding the festivities a strain because Barry was present with Ladyfriend, which did not deter him from cornering me in the hallway and pinching my derrière. Then he whispered the usual litany: Did I want to take some pictures? Did I want him back? My children would be rich someday, and I could be too. I pushed him away and tried to block him out.

"Mom, I've made a decision for us all. And it's not up for discussion.

"What's not up for discussion?"

"With our growing families, it's the only sensible thing to do."

I was waiting for the punch line.

"There will be no double birthday parties, or double holiday celebrations, or double switch-offs."

"Excuse me?" I stuttered. Then I finally figured out what he meant. Every holiday, every birthday party, every graduation in the future would include Barry and me at the same time. The conventional custom of having separate birthday parties, or alternating visits for major holidays, would be ignored.

"It simplifies things. Okay? Better go back inside now. Love ya."

I just stood there. What kind of nonsense was this? Would I really have to always socialize with my nemesis? Sit at the same table? Be reminded of my harassment so often?

My head spun.

I walked into the kitchen. Barry was there mixing a drink. I turned to back out. But not before I saw him smirk – it was obvious he had found out about the new arrangement first. Then he instantly resumed his good fellow façade, being boisterous, making silly comments, praising the seven-layer dip.

I would come home from these joint events sad and depressed. Holidays no longer gave me a modicum of enjoyment. Instead they promoted a sort of martyrdom. If it had to be, I could handle it. An orchestrated farce, if you will.

In the days before we shared celebrations, holidays had always been a strain for me. My parents would become jealous when the kids were picked up from their noonish Thanksgiving celebration and leave to go to another dinner at Barry's at 4 o'clock. Then when I was alone with Mom and Dad, they would fret out loud about Barry's more elaborate meals. They made the difficulty of watching the kids go worse. But at least I had family with me. My parents kept me from being isolated on these universal, familial occasions. Until…

My dad died suddenly while Carl and Susan were away at university. Financial stress undoubtedly had been a factor in his heart attack. He had many debts, and it became necessary for my mother to declare bankruptcy. In those days, bankruptcy was not perceived as benign as it is today. My mother and I had not a clue; Dad wanted to shelter us. We were dismayed.

My poor mother – so mindful of propriety and reputation – was mandated to appear publically in a court to be released from Dad's obligations. She displaced her negative feelings. She was congenial to others, while sharing her derogatory comments with me.

"It's all your fault," Mother began.

"How so, Mother?"

"If you hadn't married Barry and moved to California, your father would have been able to focus more on his job."

"Mother, that's not true."

"Don't disrespect me."

"I'm not. All you do is criticize my children, my job, my pets. You hurt my feelings when you call your room in my house a hole. It's what I can afford. Please, let's try to get along."

"Your dad would be shocked at your behavior."

What behavior was Mother talking about? Standing up for my life as an adult? She was lost without my dad.

Mother died a few years later of a stroke. I hadn't been in time to say goodbye to either one, to tell them I loved them and had tried so hard to please. I was now officially a senior orphan.

I wish Mother had loved me unconditionally. I wish she had known that Fig Newtons didn't really help.

As the number of my grandchildren grew, so did the shared

parties. When Ladyfriend left the room, Barry would whisper choice words to aggravate me. I tried not to listen, but that was not always possible. His words were about sex, or lack of money, or needing someone to "take care of me," emotional baby that I was. When Ladyfriend returned, Barry didn't skip a beat and resumed his jocular participation in the current conversation.

I became used to hearing, "Oh, that's just Dad…"

How did he earn a free pass?

Once Barry got caught. Carl was heading for the bathroom and saw Barry with his hands on me.

"Dad, what are you doing? Leave Mom alone."

I was mortified that Carl had seen my passivity; I should have been calling for help or at least slapping Barry. But I was apathetic as usual. I fell into old patterns of submission. I didn't have the energy to react. I didn't want a scene where Barry would spin the whole thing in his favor, no matter what. Carl stomped off with a glare. I ran after my son. Barry was unconcerned. Dare I say, rather amused.

I grabbed Carl's sleeve. "Please, I don't want any trouble."

Carl agreed to back off from Barry but couldn't promise if there were a next time. I needed my half glass of wine.

Why did I continue with this onerous schedule? Simple. I felt that if I were to absent myself, my family would stop loving me. So I continued being harassed until Barry became so angry at me that he wouldn't even acknowledge my presence. Why was he so enraged at this point in our non-relationship?

Susan would ask, "What did you do to make Dad mad?"

I couldn't speak.

Chapter 21

Through the family grapevine, I heard that Barry was having health issues. As symptoms worsened, it became apparent that he had cardiac issues, which necessitated a risky operation.

The thought of surgery was unsettling. I wouldn't wish that on anyone. And he was the father of my children.

Early on a Friday morning in May, the phone rang. I picked up the receiver before it reached the answering machine.

"Hello?"

"It's me," Barry said.

"What do you want?"

"Could you come over to my house now? I'm the only one here. I really need to see you. Trust me. It's important." There was an unusual catch in his voice that I hadn't heard before. An unfamiliar urgency.

I still didn't trust him and was afraid one of my children would drop in and think it strange to find me there. But his operation was in three days; I felt sorry for him and acquiesced.

"Give me thirty minutes," I stated.

He was listening for the bell when I arrived.

"Come in." I let myself in slowly.

He looked extremely pale and tired. I sat down on a chair opposite the sofa on which he was reclining. "Well?"

In a subdued tone, "You know that I am undergoing surgery on Monday."

"Of course, Michael told me."

"There's a chance I won't make it."

"I'm sure you'll come through okay."

"I have something to give you," he muttered. He continued with the words that would bring fleeting relief, then ruthless whiplash to my life. He left the living room and went into the den, returning a moment later with a large box. On the top he had printed my name and signed it with his. "Here," he said, in a monotone. "You can do what you want with them."

I opened the box cautiously. Inside, neatly stacked on top of each other, were staged pornographic pictures of me. I couldn't believe that he had so many left. And that he was actually giving them to me.

What was he up to? My first thought was that perhaps it was a gesture of goodwill. Because of the approaching hospital stay, he clearly didn't want anyone to stumble upon them. Was he protecting me, or himself, from our children's shock, were they to find them?

Or was this a mind game? I would be able to destroy the pictures, but he seemed unthreatened.

I was confused so I repeated, in a clear, articulate manner his offer. "I can do anything I want with them?"

"Hold them for me or get rid of them, I don't care," he clarified with an edginess creeping into his response. His mood seemed to be changing. I decided to leave before he reneged and took back the box.

The box was so heavy that he had to help me put it in the trunk of my car. I wished him good luck again and drove away, choosing to think he did love me in his own peculiar way. This was an apology for his actions.

When I arrived home, I didn't know what to do. I ran for my camera and took a picture of the closed box with my name on it as recipient and his as sender. I felt shaky. I somehow felt that I needed proof that he gave me the box. I covered it with a blanket in the trunk of the car and left it there while figuring out how to handle it.

The next morning, I called a colleague and asked her to please come over. When she asked why, I simply told her I couldn't explain over the phone.

She rang the bell forty-five minutes later.

I blushed when I told her my predicament. She led a normal married life – whatever that was. She agreed to help me get rid of the contents and promised to try to not look at the photos in the process.

Two days later, recalling the first picture barbecue with Derek, we lit the small grill in my backyard. It was a hot summer day, and the smoldering pictures generated a lot of smoke. We were so scared of burning, we did it a little at a time, like we were somehow the guilty ones. It seemed to take forever. Then we heard a helicopter and actually went to hide, thinking someone had sent them to see what we were doing.

I kept two pictures from when I was just married, and crying. If I had to reveal the circumstances of our relationship later on, for whatever reason, I would have tangible proof of his coercion.

The sad fact was that if he had not given me verbal permission to do what I wanted with the box, I wouldn't have been brave enough to destroy the prints. I was so locked into being intimidated that I thought Barry might take me to court for destroying his property. But I couldn't afford to bypass this opportunity. I might never have another.

I had the pictures. But I didn't register that the plethora of home movies was still missing.

Barry made it through the risky procedure. I was relieved, for I did not wish that sort of grievous ending for anyone. I naively thought that the blackmail was over, once and for all. Perhaps the medical trauma had changed him for the better.

Therefore three months later, when he called and asked me to meet him for lunch, I accepted. He said he wanted to talk about the children.

At noon we met at a moderately crowded Denny's, choosing a table near the pastry display. I figured I could always focus on cream puffs and éclairs. Our conversation started in a quasi-friendly manner. He was looking well, and I told him so. I even inquired about Ladyfriend.

Then I asked him the reason for this meeting.

For a moment, I noticed a fleeting look of anger. Maybe I was mistaken about his motives being benign.

He got right to the point. "I want my pictures back."

"Excuse me?"

"I want my pictures back. They were in the box you were holding for me. When can I pick them up?"

I was shocked. "I don't have them anymore. When you told me I could do what I wanted, I got rid of them."

"I don't believe you," he threatened.

I remembered that tone of voice – remembered all too well. I felt nervous again. "You told me I could do anything I wanted with them. You were afraid the operation might go poorly. You gave them back to me. I appreciated that."

"Give me a break! I want my pictures back!" His voice was rising, and several diners turned toward our table.

"Please lower your voice," I whispered. "The pictures are gone. I do not have them anymore."

"Where are they?"

"I, I burned them. A friend helped me," I mumbled.

"I don't believe you," he repeated.

I felt nauseated. I was still afraid of him. I knew then that he hadn't changed at all. It was indeed a new mind game.

"Where are my pictures?"

Thereafter, at every subsequent family gathering, he found a time to whisper in my ear, "Where are my pictures? I want them back."

I dropped out of the dating scene. I was just too weary and wary. I concentrated on trying to be more assertive with others in daily life, including my children. If an introverted person suddenly dissents or gives a true opinion, all hell breaks out. People are so confounded that they feel compelled to squelch the comment and rally around the contradicted party. I tried to expose Barry's true nature. Both instances were at holiday dinners. Both backfired.

My first attempt was at a Christmas Eve celebration. Before we sat down to dinner, I had been taunted with the customary "you owe me pictures," in a quasi-jocular tone. Then Barry slapped me on the back. When we sat down, he made a joke about my parenting, pointedly referring to my finances or lack thereof. I had consumed my limit of a half glass of wine, and words slithered out of my mouth.

"Well, what kind of father talks about de-virginizing his own daughter?"

I was mortified. I couldn't believe I had trespassed into forbidden territory. My daughter was present, and I had never openly referred to anything off color. All my children were listening. I waited for the axe to fall.

It didn't.

All I heard was an, "Oh, that's just Dad being Dad. He has a queer, quirky sense of humor."

Everyone seemed to concur. The moment passed with no repercussions. After all, Dad was joking.

At another gathering, Michael, unfortunately, was contemplating a divorce. He of the no-double-celebrations. For a reason that I have blocked out, I asked Michael, if he did split up, would he continue his strict familial policy? I had barely finished when his siblings jumped on me for upsetting him when he was having difficulties. That was it. I'd learned my lesson. I even apologized to my own children.

I had waited too long for outing the truth. Like the identity of "Deep Throat," so much time had passed it seemed like no one was really interested anymore. The passage of time does that.

ANA RÊVE

Chapter 22

Several years later, Barry started feeling ill again.

In his recovery period, he bought a house in a new development behind Susan's. They had a mutual fence in the backyard; he could use a ladder to climb onto her property. Barry was living a dream of mine. I adored my daughter and wanted to live next door to her and her family. She always saw the good in people. As it was, I lived nearby but also wanted her away from Barry's questionable influence. I was so jealous. My heart clenched when Barry usurped my vision.

Barry's Ladyfriend moved into the new home. On the outside, Barry appeared a nice guy. I became plagued by the notion that he treated only me poorly. At a subsequent Thanksgiving dinner held at their house, I noticed that Ladyfriend had her own bedroom. I wondered why. I had so many questions I wanted to ask her, but as usual, I didn't dare pry. Maybe there was a legitimate reason – maybe she snored. I really wanted her to say that she and Barry had a platonic relationship because she too had found his sexual appetite excessive and unpalatable. That would make me feel better.

I mastered the façade of indifference, molding my sensitivity into stone. I felt that I could stand anything, no matter how uncomfortable, for an hour or two.

I concentrated on pets and novels, deciding to be content with simple pleasures.

Susan and her husband were vacationing in Yosemite. She had asked me to water her plants while she was gone, bring in the paper and mail at least every other day. Mainly Susan wanted me to check on her cats. She knew I was aware of their actions, especially around doors: cats were escape artists, ready to bolt. On one particular morning, I had just started my rounds, when I heard the lock turn in the front door. My daughter had given her father a key in case of an emergency, as I found out later. She had just called him to check if some workers had access to the backyard. They were installing a fountain and she couldn't remember if she had unlocked the side gate.

When the door opened and Barry walked in, I froze, panicked.

How to describe his expression? He had probably seen my car, so he was aware of my presence. His lips were smiling, but his eyes weren't.

I put down my watering can, grabbed my purse, and started for the door. He caught my arm.

"Where do you think you're going?" he asked. "I call this a stroke of fate."

"Please let go of my arm." I hated the quiver in my voice. I had spent years exploring how to become less submissive. I resolved to take charge of the situation and channeled my courage. "I'm leaving now."

"No you're not. Sorry, it's a stroke of fate," he repeated.

He blocked my way. I tried again to be forceful.

"If you put your hands on me again, I'll call a lawyer and sue you for harassment," I declared. "Times have changed, you know."

"Not for you," he said.

So then I played my trump card. I reminded him of Ladyfriend. How upset she would be if he were to fool around with another woman, if that indeed were his intent.

He laughed. And proceeded condescendingly to explain, as he put it, in a way that I could understand. He was immune to any vulnerability. He reminded me of his wealth, my limited means, and his subsequent power to hire the best attorneys. He threatened me with going to the school where I taught and creating a scandal. My professional life had been the one area in which I found peace. My head started to pound.

He concluded with an ace up his sleeve. "It would be your word against mine. An emotional baby against a retired, successful CPA. Two divorces, overly-controlled childhood, and a background of seeing a shrink. Borderline anorexic to boot. No one would believe you. Money is power, and I have lots of money. Therefore I have lots of power. Checkmate."

I knew he was right. At first, I couldn't even react when he reached out to pull me towards him. I recoiled.

He chanted, "F-A-T-E."

I managed a "Please, no."

He tightened his grip on my arm. My former feelings of helplessness flooded through my body. It looked like he was going to kiss me, and I reflexively started to gag. Even after all this time. I jump-started my out of body mind-control. It would be over soon.

Suddenly, I got mad. The past was the past. This was the present. I was no longer a victim. In fact, I was a survivor. I stepped back and knocked his hand off me.

"No! Don't you dare!"

Barry was stunned. He started reaching towards me again, then stopped midway. I saw a flicker of weakness, a tinge of fear, in his eyes.

I stomped to the front door, grabbed my purse, my adrenaline at high pitch. I had stood up to him.

The last words he said to me were, "You broke up our family. You can still come back."

I slammed that front door behind me.

The first thing I did when I got home was take a shower. I was shaking but proud, trying to force the possible consequences of my actions out of my mind. I knew I would disintegrate in court; I couldn't endure rounds of he-said-she-said. I remembered that girl thrown into a non-consensual dark world of extreme sexual demands. I, so shy, who had not been allowed to lock the bathroom door in the early days of our marriage, an only child who valued privacy to a fault: I felt strong. My yesterdays would not return to haunt me as forcefully.

I had been able to stand up for myself. I had not caved in to Barry's threats.

A small step forward that I kept to myself.

Chapter 23

Slowly Barry was becoming paterfamilias of the family. His non-participation in his progeny's childhood seemed merely innocuous to them. Oh well. Was it his money? It certainly was not his personality, with its spiteful teasing. Maybe he was different when I wasn't around.

I resented it, this paterfamilias posture. So, at last, I started skipping some holidays.

In spite of myself, I did miss my parents. In a strange way, Mother had lived a very sheltered life because of my compliance and Dad's unconditional support. I wish she had hugged or kissed me just once for the sheer joy of it. But now, especially on holidays with streets deserted and restaurants closed, I admitted I still wanted her around.

I missed my dad. Those childhood carousel rides had been so

important to me; it was our time together. I knew he loved me and had fond memories of our jaunts. However, Dad had never been able to gain entry to a different social class. And my choice of men was like a betrayal.

I eventually got used to being alone on the holidays. It was better than the alternative. My pets kept me company, my cat purred. I pretended not to care about my isolation for so long that I finally believed it. If truth be told, I did care in my heart. So I made my holidays into school workdays. It took discipline. I had plenty of school work to do.

No tenure in the private sector kept me on my toes and vulnerable. My parents had relentlessly urged me to transfer to the public school system for better benefits and a higher salary. They had been right. Because in my late sixties, unbelievably, I was still worried about water heaters failing, infamous PG&E bills, and the like. I still felt like a struggling college student. I was used to struggling. Money doesn't buy happiness, but it sure takes away the what-if-it-breaks and leaky roof worries.

Nonetheless, I was all right. I had actively removed myself from finding a male companion. I had tried one last time with a lawyer who checked my refrigerator because he didn't believe in expiration dates on milk, cottage cheese, and yogurt. Immediately I chose not to take a chance on him or another man for financial security.

So I hung around with my black flat coated retriever, Shasta. I had owned many dogs, but she was special. I couldn't imagine life without her. She was my antidote to problems. I could unwind with her. I didn't have to worry, or defend myself, or apologize for no reason. I had spent so much time avoiding confrontation: yes, I had seen a shrink; yes, I had been dominated by my parents; yes, I was single and on the borderline financially. So be it. I had Shasta. And a job. And a young rescue mutt, and my kitties. And my children and grandchildren.

I'd be okay.

Chapter 24

In the fall of 2008, I was running around as usual. Papers to grade, students' parents to call, mundane chores, walks with my dogs. Shasta was getting old, and I was trying to block out the fact that she was almost sixteen. She had arthritis and stomach problems. Too bad that dogs and humans have to deteriorate in old age. I psyched myself out to take it day by day. My thoughts were permeated by willing her to miraculously improve. So when Susan had mentioned that Barry was in the hospital, the true magnitude of that statement – a serious relapse – didn't penetrate my consciousness. I had not spoken with him for months.

Around Thanksgiving, I was getting ready for bed when I heard a crash. It was Shasta falling. She couldn't stand up. She had suffered a stroke. I begged her to get up. She couldn't. She looked at me with her beautiful eyes as if to say, "Goodbye. Don't cry. I love you." I called Carl and Susan. By morning Shasta was gone.

I'm not sure that anyone really understood the scope of my loss.

My beloved dog died, and the world went about its business. Which, I know, is as it should be. I was no novice in the loss of pets. Somehow this one was the most wrenching. I reread "*The Rainbow Bridge*." I reread Jack London's analogy from *Call of the Wild:* "It [death] left a great void in him, somewhat akin to hunger, but a void which ached and ached and which food could not fill."

I was numb. My students helped keep me focused. In fact, they would time my crying spurts and record the duration of each episode, waiting and hoping for a reduction in minutes. My rescue dog kept me company.

Two weeks passed…

I was in my usual rush. I had to prepare a test for the next day. I dashed from my bedroom to the kitchen where I had left my text. In the hallway, I tripped over a dog toy and flipped over. Landing on my back, I knew that I was in trouble. I couldn't move, and the pain was excruciating. My dog was licking my face and whimpering. Using all my willpower, I slid on my back to the kitchen and pulled myself up by clutching a chair leg to reach the phone cord. I managed to call my daughter, who called her brothers. Twenty-five minutes later, I was on my way to the emergency room, being transported from car to hospital on a lawn chair.

After painful x-rays and consultations, the diagnosis: I had broken my right hip. I kept sobbing and whimpering, "This can't be happening. I have to go home." I was shot up with morphine.

The next day, a Friday, I underwent surgery. By Monday I wasn't doing well and developed a mysterious fever resistant to antibiotics.

The doctor couldn't assure my family that I would pull through. I was suddenly facing my own mortality. I overheard the medical staff whispering about my condition outside the door.

At that very same time of my hospitalization, Barry was in a room two floors below. He had been there for a week. I hadn't processed that Barry could be so ill. For the past six months, I had heard bits and pieces about Barry's hospital stays and subsequent recoveries. I had accepted the latest smidgen of information from Susan and falsely concluded that it was a recurring medical pattern that would ultimately turn out okay. Through my feverish haze I now understood that Barry was terminally ill.

My children took turns running up and down to watch over their dad, then stand vigil over me. It felt surreal.

Barry succumbed while I was running the unexplained fever. I was told of his passing and couldn't fully absorb the thought. My mind was overtaken by fear of my own infection and possible additional surgery. I was so sick and afraid that I wouldn't make it.

There was a memorial service for Barry the next day. Obviously I could not attend. Therefore his demise was a vague, *did-I-really-hear-it?* memory. There was no closure. I should have been at Barry's funeral. He was the father of my children. There were so many questions that would remain unanswered. Why did we stay together? Did he love me, albeit in his own perverted way? Did he really believe I hadn't destroyed the box of pictures?

The timing was bizarre: Barry's loss and my hospitalization. The coincidence of our joint hospital stay, even now as I reflect upon it: What were the odds? I remember the timing of my second marriage and appendicitis. And, of course, there was the ill-fated timing of the chance meeting while house-sitting. So many coincidences. What do

I make of it, this pattern? Some message from on high? Was this my barefoot trial over hot coals? I just don't know.

My fever broke several days later.

Rehabilitation was slow. For three weeks I had to depend on Susan to look after me and take care of the animals. I was afraid of falling again and embarrassed to use the walker. I hated being dependent on others. I did, however, luck out with a homecare person who loved animals.

When I was given the go-ahead to start driving, I was too jittery to begin. I had to be coached and treated with kid gloves for short distances, gradually building up to a grocery run. Michael, especially, encouraged me during this phase.

Meanwhile I had to take a six month obligatory leave of absence from teaching – the main constant in my life. I would have to decide if it was time to retire. My aches and pains reminded me that literally overnight I had become a true senior. I felt self-conscious walking with a cane. Before the fall, I had always felt like a recycled teenager, cavorting around class to make a point to my junior high students. Now my mortality accompanied me everywhere.

As the time came closer to resolve my immediate future, I felt a buildup of anxiety. I wanted to continue teaching. However, I was starting to feel strange. Disoriented. Shaky. Restless. I had to keep moving. I circled the living room, sometimes for hours. I had difficulty concentrating. I knew I needed to stop moving – I was getting tired – yet I was incapable of stopping this odd, repetitious behavior.

My spirit was willing to resume educating, but I could no longer trust my body. I was terrified of falling again. What if a student bumped into me? Or I was hit by a dodge ball?

I have a newfound respect and empathy for disabled persons. I see an elderly lady using a walker and understand the ramifications of her situation. When I had to use a walker, I was very disturbed. I wanted to skip my required therapy. I wanted to hide my weakness, an arrow catapulting towards mortality. Now I smile and engage in small talk with a person pushing a walker. I get it. It's a humbling experience. It is true that there can be no empathy unless you share the same experience – sympathy yes, empathy no.

Chapter 25

During my compulsive, circular path, I remembered the two photos I had kept – ones from when I was a new bride, saved in case no one would believe me about my life. They were the least explicit, yet not quite tame enough for public viewing. An exhibit, so to speak, of my veracity. There was an accompanying small notebook, noting some of the more traumatic events in my marriage, started when Barry claimed that I was the one who broke up the family. Suddenly, I panicked. I did not want my children to see these items. In my gut, I was afraid that my display would somehow backfire. How to get rid of them? Preferably, immediately?

My close friend was visiting me, quite concerned about my erratic behavior and my fragile state of mind.

"How can I help you?" she asked.

I handed her the items. Another burning – only on a stovetop, not a grill, this time. At her home. *Plus ça change, plus c'est la même chose.*

I felt better for a moment.

Then my doubt and restlessness returned. Should I have kept the proof?

I was unnerved, restless. I couldn't stop circling my living room. Something was amiss. I felt disoriented. Unbeknownst to me at the time I had an acute bladder infection, which sometimes leads to delirium. Eventually I couldn't focus on any type of reading material or TV; it was then that I knew I was in big trouble.

The series of emotional and physical disturbances resulted in extreme stress; it was too much for me. My beloved Shasta had died. I broke my hip. Barry died in the same hospital. At the same time, my teaching career was a question mark. My life was spinning out of control. All my time-worn compartments fell out of the dresser as if displaced by an earthquake. A heap of debris. A mixed-up stack of seemingly insoluble problems.

An overload. Four major traumas in a small space of time. I was functioning on the outside, but floundering on the inside.

I had an anxiety-ridden breakdown…

It took several months to find the correct medication to treat my acute disquietude. Unfortunately, my original meds had produced adverse side effects, making for a longer recuperation. My children took turns checking up on me.

One morning, while lying on the couch in the living room, I heard the phone ring in the kitchen and Susan answered. It was Susan's former roommate calling to catch up.

After the usual pleasantries, I heard Susan say, "Mom's having a rough time. Dad was right when he stated Mom needed him to take care of her. She asked for a divorce when she met a cute young guy. He said it wouldn't last. Her second marriage fell through. Dad had told me he knew the 60/40 arrangement would never work. Mom just needed him to take care of her. Dad had plenty of money. Mom broke up the family for no reason. Whatever. I know one thing, I'll never get divorced."

The mild, matter-of-fact comment – Dad perceived as my only true benefactor – spurred me on to let the truth be told. It was the last straw. I needed to set the record straight. I didn't want to enable a false legacy.

Facing my own mortality had changed me. I had never thought about legacies, about how I would be remembered.

Years of abuse. And I was the culpable party? No way. I had been protecting my family. Now it was time to protect myself.

So I started to write my life story.

When I arrived at the final chapters, I hesitated. My thoughts scattered. Will there be a happy or unhappy ending to this mini-saga?

Choices.

I could finally meet my (now-aging) Prince Charming. He'd be kind, generous, love animals, and buy fresh produce.

I could become a self-imposed pariah and withdraw from society like Emily Dickinson.

I could warn all women of distorted dreams, a veritable harbinger of marital doom and gloom.

I can laugh with others at myself because in this day and age, my abuse and blackmail seem, well, a non-shocker—if not bland in this technological era of sexting and anything goes.

I can send out a memo to women that what appears to be unbridled desire is really a lust for power.

Or I can just continue with my pledge to never let down or betray a promise to a child. To give them unconditional love. That which I never experienced, and longed for all my life.

I can be philosophical: Is Money power? Absolutely. Does it surpass Love? Most likely. And, what about Forgiveness? What about it?

The dilemma I have with forgiveness is the notion of time. Most of the self-help tomes laud letting go of anger. Then supposedly one can find peace and march fearlessly into the sunset.

But wait, a ray of hope. A few days ago, I met a very eligible man. He was enjoying a cup of coffee outside Peets. He had a beautiful Great Pyrenees at his feet. He asked if I wanted to join him at the table with his dog. I guess he noticed the way I looked at the delicious white canine. "May I offer him a treat?" I asked.

"Of course, we love treats. And pretty girls."

At that moment, I felt the rush of excitement. This guy was the right age, sounded literate, loved dogs, and was quite good looking. In his early 70s, he still had a twinkle in his blue eyes. His grey hair complemented a small goatee which added to his rakish look. His hand rested on his dog's head while he told me he was a Berkeley grad with a major in American history. His pluses were multiplying. At that moment, I forgot that now I was Andrew Lloyd Webber's old cat in the sun, from "Memory."

That long forgotten sexual tension bubbled up. He reminded me of a Kenny Rogers type. I could be his "lady." Maybe I wasn't outdated. Maybe I should try again. Inside I was more seventeen than seventy. I started feeling the adrenaline high. I consciously opted for passion.

I let him buy me a skinny vanilla latte. It turned out that he lived in an apartment complex within walking distance. I didn't have my dogs with me, so I agreed to accompany him home to play ball with his pup. When he took my hand, I shivered even though it was seventy-eight degrees.

His apartment was on the second floor. He asked me to wait outside the door for five minutes so he could tidy up quickly. I had my Kindle Fire with me and was only too happy to comply.

I heard soft music being turned on.

Finally he opened the door, motioning for me to enter. I noted the stereotypical bachelor pad. Large, comfy, faux-leather sofa sprinkled with white fur. His dog, Duke, galumphed towards me and started covering my hands with slurpy kisses. I loved it. Kenny Look-alike headed to the kitchen for wine. He returned and set two filled glasses on an Ikea coffee table.

I stood up. I had been hunkering down with Duke.

Kenny decided we needed some snacks too. He would forage in the fridge.

"Almost there, darling," he whispered.

"Take your time. Duke, where's your ball?"

Duke left the room to search for his toy.

I heard the refrigerator door slam, a cupboard opening, silverware clinking.

Kenny reappeared with a tray. He placed it next to our drinks.

I looked over his shoulder at the hors d'oeuvres. I began to tremble.

He smiled and opened his arms.

I ran.

Out the door.

Back into the hallway.

Back down the stairs, remembering to hold onto the banister.

Back to my car.

No more.

On that tray? Triscuits bordering Brie. If that wasn't a sign, what was?

Had it been Ritz bordering Feta, I might have stayed.

www.ingramcontent.com/pod-product-compliance
Lightning Source LLC
Chambersburg PA
CBHW060328260626
47160CB00007B/2724